A Zealot's
Redemption

Brennan,

I'm so glad to have you
are in our Life of Christ Class.
God Bless You,

Ray Adams

A Zealot's Redemption

A Novel

Ray Adams

Author's Note

FOR MANY YEARS my students and friends have encouraged me to write a book about the time of Jesus that would encapsulate some of the stories of His life from the Gospels in a creative way. I decided to write a historical fiction that would present Jesus as the Son of God and the Savior of the world, but in a readable story with some twists.

During my 42 years as a Professor at Baptist Bible College in Springfield, MO, I have approached the study of Biblical History by encouraging my students to allow their minds to gravitate to the past as they studied the Old and New Testaments. Try to place yourself in the setting of every story and watch the events unfold. As all of my students come to understand, (I hope), it is important to bridge some gaps to better understand the context of the

Bible. I've encouraged them to bridge their knowledge of external information about the setting of all Biblical stories to the best of their abilities.

I want my students to be able to bridge the *Historical Gap.*

Apart from what the Bible tells us, which is the most important part, what do we know about the history of that time period and the events that were going on? What God gives us in His Holy Bible is inspired and totally true, but sometimes there is historical information that supplements our knowledge of what is taking place in and around the Biblical story.

Another area my students should bridge is the *Language Gap.*

The Bible was written in ancient languages that we seldom speak or use now. Therefore, it is important for us to understand the nuances of those languages and unique words. There are wonderful academic tools that help us glean information about the words God selected to use when He gave us His Word through holy men of old. That is also why I encourage Bible students to consider taking language studies such as Greek or Hebrew so they can better understand the distinctions of those words.

I want my students to also bridge the *Cultural Gap.*

As best they are able, I want them to understand what things were like culturally in the Biblical period of the narrative. For example, the Bible talks about *leprosy.* We don't know much about that dreaded disease, but to understand how the Jewish people reacted to those with leprosy, helps us comprehend why some of the stories about it developed the way they did. Bridging the *Cultural Gap* makes our understanding of the stories even better.

Then, I want my budding scholars to be able to bridge the *Geography Gap.*

Having hosted or led more than 20 tours to the Holy Land, I understand one of the great values of going to Israel is to be able to visualize the geography and topography of the lands of the Bible. It is one of the most impactful things people take away from such a trip. They often comment that they never read their Bible the same way because they now can visualize what those places and settings look like. One such pilgrim made this statement about his Bible comprehension which so resonated with me. He said, "I have new eyes." That's the power of bridging the *Geography Gap.*

I have found that when my students learn to bridge the *Historical Gap, Language Gap, Cultural Gap,* and *Geography Gap,* they are armed with information that will supplement their understanding of the Bible. After fleshing out all of those various details, they can come to almost any biblical passage and put it in its proper historical and grammatical context. Then all a person has to do is read the text and comprehend, *Oh, I see what God is saying here.*

That is the most liberating experience in your personal Bible study.

So, I have brought this approach to my work of fiction. Most of the details are rooted and based in historical facts that set the stage for this historical novel. I have certainly taken some literary license with some parts of the narrative. Most of the characters are fictional, although there are numerous biblical actors who are very real from history-- especially Jesus.

Before you begin reading this book I would like to say Thank You to several people who made this an enjoyable experience. Again, many of my students have encouraged and pushed me to do this work.

I appreciated my wife, Beth, and her inspiration, patience and encouragement to allow me to create this book. She was one of my editors and one of my biggest supporters during this process.

I have numerous friends and colleagues at Baptist Bible College and in the ministry who have expressed their deep support. I want to thank my friends, Bill Levergood, Dana Beck, and Sherman Pridham for proofing the drafts and making edits and recommendations.

My daughter-in-law, Lisa, shared some important thoughts while reading the early drafts. My granddaughter, Adrian, who is only 16, provided some of my most valuable and creative suggestions. She has all the makings of an excellent future editor.

I also want to thank my long-time friend, David Stokes, accomplished author, editor, and publisher. He guided me through this process with strong suggestions, coaching, and valuable editing to help polish the final product. He created *Critical Mass Publishing* which has helped facilitate the production of the book.

So let's begin with an important introduction that gives some of the historical background and context for the story you will read...

Ray Adams
Springfield, Missouri
August 2020

INTRODUCTION

It's A Roman World

THIS IS A work of historical fiction. The background story for my story is essential to understanding the story itself. So, before we plunge into the narrative, let me explain a little about the historical context.

Politics--It's been been around since the time of Creation. I've heard it said that the word itself comes from the Greek; *Poli,* meaning "many, and; "*Ticks,* meaning, "blood sucking creatures." Throughout history, politics has influenced the rise and fall of civilizations. There are those who have power and those who are oppressed. There are the wealthy and those who struggle for daily food to eat. There are the *Nobles* and there are peasants. There are High Priests and laymen. There are Kings and Subjects.

Politics is in every level of society and government. Who will control? Who will acquiesce? This has been the common process from time immemorial.

Power. Strength. Dominance.

In the first century of the Christian era, the pendulum of power and submission was clearly fixed against the background of the "Pax Romana" or the Period of Roman Peace (31 BC - 180 AD). The Rome dominated the Mediterranean Basin, and her influence stretched from North Africa to the Germanic Tribes of North-Eastern Europe and all the way to the Atlantic Ocean in Western Europe. The Parthian World in the regions of the Old Persian Empire stood as a lonely and stubborn holdout to Rome's ever-expanding power eastward. In 31 BC, at the crucial naval Battle of Actium, Octavian, the nephew and adopted son of Julius Caesar, crushed the alliance between Marc Antony and his consort, Cleopatra of Egypt.

These North African rebels had set their designs on taking over the Roman Republic and making it a united kingdom under their auspices. But when Octavian routed the forces of Antony, his one time friend turned rival, everything changed. Antony perished in the conflict, and when Cleopatra realized her hopeless fate she allegedly committed suicide rather than face certain humiliation. With no other rivals in the Roman Republic, the Senators yielded their already waning power and insisted that the great conqueror Octavian assume the persona of Augustus Caesar.

With the Republic abolished, the Senators established, Imperial Rome, with Augustus Caesar as their first Emperor--for life. Augustus ushered in a period of military dominance, control, and affluence that led to more than 200 years without major conflict within the Empire. Hence, the Pax Romana.

These political machinations forever changed the course of human history.

In a small, inconspicuous, and unimportant Province of the Empire, called Judea, located along the eastern coast of the Mediterranean Sea in the former Seleucid Empire of Syria, submission to Roman authority involved intense oppression.

Judea had been added to the Roman Republic as a Province when General Pompey, a member of the First Triumvirate along with Julius Caesar, conquered Jerusalem in 63 BC. This area was deemed strategically important by the Romans so they set up a series of client Kings to represent them in that obscure part of the world. In this tiny outpost of the massive Roman Empire, politics played a major role as Judea became an emerging hotspot for resistance. Many forces were at work, forces that would create circumstances which would impact world history.

Judea needed a steady hand, and a ruthless one if necessary, to secure Roman dominance. The Romans had found such an ally in the region with an Idumean ruler named, Antipater. He had originally established himself as a military man in the areas south and east of the Dead Sea. In the former biblical lands of Moab and Edom, Antipater gained recognition as a trusted ally of the burgeoning Roman world. During the period of the Republic, Antipater was acknowledged as a capable friend of Rome. But forces were at work to challenge Antipater and his family, as well as his assistance to Rome.

A group of rebels started guerilla attacks against the forces of Antipater, and their tactics and growing strength threatened stability in the region. The success of these rebel challengers drew outside forces to supply them with finances and weapons. The kingdom that benefitted most from this subterfuge was the Parthian Empire, on the eastern border of the Republic. Financed by Parthian monies, the Idumean rebels started hitting the Antipater dynasty very hard. In fact, the resistance made a decisive attack resulting in Antipater's death, as well as that of his oldest son, Phasael. When this happened, the surviving son of Antipater--a man called Herod--escaped the region with his life, making his way to Rome to seek support.

While he was still alive and an influencer in Rome, Marc Antony decided to become Herod's benefactor and actually brought him before the Roman Senate to bestow upon him a title and the backing required to recapture the territories that the Idumean insurgents had taken when they killed Antipater. The Roman Senate, desiring to strengthen their eastern frontier by having loyal client nobles in strategic positions, agreed to Antony's proposal. In 40 BC, the Roman Senate bestowed upon Herod a special honor and title.

"King of the Jews!"

Now this maneuver was both savvy and strategic, and it seemed logical for the Romans. But it overlooked one crucial political detail. The ultra-orthodox Jewish people were expectant that a new King--their Messiah, born from the linage of their greatest monarch, King David, 1000 years earlier--would soon establish a new Jewish Monarchy. So when Herod was appointed by the Roman Senate as the "King of the Jews," Jewish acceptance was very much in question. This man wasn't even a Jew. How could he be their King?

But Rome wanted their vassal King on the front lines, and a slight offense to the Jewish religion didn't seem like that big of a deal. Interestingly, when Herod went back to Judea to firmly establish his regime, he came to recognize that his supporter and benefactor, Marc Antony, was charting a course with Cleopatra that seemed destined to fail. As Antony's coup intentions became more and more apparent, Herod cleverly shifted his allegiance to Octavian because he realized the catastrophe that was about to befall the doomed couple with Empire building aspirations. So when the debacle at Actium played out, and Octavian accepted the life-long title of Emperor Augustus Caesar, Herod was shrewdly on the right side of the new Roman Empire. He had aligned himself with a winner, and it allowed Herod to stay in power until his death.

Another issue plagued Herod's initial kingdom building. Among the Jewish people there had been a fleeting hope that, indeed, the Davidic Kingdom and their long-awaited Messiah were about to become a reality. Following what many people considered a miraculous Maccabean victory over the pagan Seleucid Monarch, Antiochus IV Epiphanes, in 164 BC, the Maccabean family line established a brief, royal kingdom named after a Maccabean ancestor, Hashmon.

The Dynasty was called the Hasmoneans.

The Jewish people saw in this a clear path to their independence and a dynasty that would culminate with their Messiah. Then suddenly, General Pompey came with his crushing Roman legions and subjugated the Judean territory, making it part of the Roman Republic in 63 BC. The dramatic Messianic hope that had so fueled the Jews now seemed improbable, if not impossible. Herod ruled the Jews even though he knew little about them. But he understood politics and power. He exacted merciless punishment on those who dared oppose him.

In one horrific action at the beginning of his reign, Herod returned from Rome with the backing of the most powerful military might in the world. To show his total control, Herod, rounded up 45 prominent Hasmoneans' and had them executed to demonstrate his dominance and remove any possible rival--royal family members who might one day attempt to foment insurrection against him.

The Jewish people were appalled. The brutality immediately communicated the kind of ruthlessness Herod would impose to secure his vassal kingdom. He also tried to establish a Hasmonean link to his own monarchy by marrying a beautiful woman who was a princess from the Jewish dynasty. Her name was Mariamne, and she was Herod's "First Ranked Wife." Herod loved her more than any of his other wives from politically motivated marriages. Yet even his favorite wife, Mariamne, would not be spared an ignominious death that befell anyone suspected of disloyalty or rebellion against the insecure and paranoid monarch.

One thing Herod did very well was build. He built new cities. He built new temples. And he built several important fortresses around his kingdom. The first and most pragmatic was the fortress of Antonia built right next to the Temple of God in Jerusalem. Both Herod and the Romans believed that if insurrection was going to come from the Jews, it was going to find its impetus from their main worship center, the Temple. So Herod built a fortress where the Romans could garrison their troops during Holidays and Feast Days. Normally, the Roman troops were housed at their headquarters in Caesarea Marittima, along the Mediterranean Sea. Herod was the one who built Caesarea Marittima and named it in honor of the Emperor. Antonia was named after his initial supporter, Marc Antony, but Herod's loyalties were, again, squarely in support of his new patron, Augustus.

Many of Herod's other building projects gained him a reputation of being a creative and masterful architect. Of all Herod's construction projects, his most costly and magnanimous enterprise was the remodeling of the Jewish Second Temple in Jerusalem. It was not a new Temple as some people believe, but rather an *expansion* of the Temple complex. The Second Temple was remodeled with many amazing features and costly upgrades. Much of it was covered with gold and other priceless materials. It glimmered in the abundant sunlight around the hills of Jerusalem and made the Jewish people swell with pride. Their Temple gained worldwide notoriety for its extravagant beauty.

In spite of Herod's efforts to win the favor of his Jewish subjects by remodeling their primary shrine, they still resisted his role as the "King of the Jews." He was an outsider who supported and built other pagan shrines in other places in the Roman world. But it was his beautiful reconstruction of the Second Temple of God that primarily earned him the sobriquet he is known for in history.

"Herod, The Great!"

It was into this politically charged setting that events began to play out that would forever reshape the course of history. Many of these changes would find their impetus in the northern regions of Judea--an area called Galilee.

A Zealot's
Redemption

CHAPTER ONE

A Zealot is Born

SIMEON OF CANA quietly and anxiously awaited his fate. He had resigned himself to the inevitable. He was going to be executed by a group of Roman soldiers.

It was because of that one, ill-fated, decision to fulfill a vow that now he stood condemned. He racked his brain trying to figure out how he could have handled things differently. His life, family, and hope were all going to be forfeited because of one disastrous moment.

Okay, it was really a series of events that had brought him to his doom. As is often the case, the choice of friends can determine our future. But this outcome had been in the making for many years. Simeon rehearsed in his mind the circumstances that had brought him to this moment of

personal calamity. His thoughts gravitated to the past even
as he faced his ominous future. He started to replay his
memories of when he was a young boy growing up in
Galilee.

Thirty years ago.

One of his earliest memories was the tragic death of
his father, Eleazar. Simeon was about eight years old when
the shocking news came. Needless to say, growing up as a
fatherless child to a widowed mother was a terrible
experience in First Century Judea. His mother Miriam
tried her best to provide for the children and fortunately,
there were grandparents in the area that helped when they
could. Still, the challenges of growing up without a father
and a mentor was a crushing blow to an impressionable
boy

Raised in the little Galilean village of Cana, Simeon
and his little sister and brother were from the region of the
old Israelite tribal territories of Naphtali and Ashur-- not
far from the Sea of Galilee. His father had been a deeply
religious man who always took the family to Synagogue. He
was a devout man who regularly taught his children the
Shema, Moses' lofty acknowledgment of the Jewish
monotheistic religion found in the Torah, as well as other
important Jewish laws.

Standard issue in an orthodox home.

Eleazar had identified with a small, but zealous group
of Jews in Galilee, who were excited and expectant that the
Messiah would soon come to overthrow the Romans and
establish a new Kingly line in the tradition of the great King
David. In fact, Eleazar was so passionate about his beliefs
that he had joined a group of Jewish Nationalists who
believed they could accelerate the coming of the Messiah
by harassing and resisting the Roman occupation.

This affiliation led to his untimely demise.

As Simeon approached his tenth birthday, he began asking his mother more and more questions about his father's death. The boy had seen his mother struggling to feed him and his siblings since becoming a widow. Not only was life harshly complicated, but Simeon had also seen the utter disappointment and grief his mother endured. It made him so sad, but it fueled his desire to know more about his father' death.One day Simeon just blurted out, "How did Abba die? Is it true he was killed by the Romans?" Miriam was somewhat startled by his bold questions, but she tried her best to give him an answer.

"Your father was a very good man and he provided for us very nicely. He was a hardworking man and he was a master stonemason," she said. "Everyone knew of his quality work. He was sought after for his expertise and even had to travel from Cana to Capernaum, Sepphoris, Nazareth, and Nain to do work for people. They all praised his quality craftsmanship, and he was recommended to many other people."

"Wow," Simeon responded. "He really was a great man. But how did he die? Why would the Romans kill my father if he was such a good man?"

Miriam tried to select her words wisely, "Well, your father also loved Jehovah with a great passion. He was zealous that God and God alone be worshipped, but the growing Roman influence here in the Galilee brought many pagan and ungodly people to this area. Even though he hated working there sometimes, Sepphoris was the headquarters of the Roman soldiers in this region and their growing community provided many opportunities for work. Even the Romans appreciated your father's masonry expertise. Many of the foreigners liked your dad and his friendly ways."

She paused, as if lost in thought, then continued, "He would frequently come home after long hours and even days away from all of us, and he would be grieved over the idolatry and paganism he often saw among the Roman occupiers. He didn't like to be around them but the money was good and your father wanted to provide for his family so he endured the lamentable conditions when working around the Romans."

Simeon continued to press, "But why did those people who liked him want to kill him?"

Miriam tried to explain her husband's burden for God to be the King for the Jewish people and that He alone was to be honored. She attempted to bring these most profound theological concepts down to a level a ten-year-old could grasp.

"Eleazar started assembling with a man named Judas of Galilee, and other like-minded Jewish patriots, including our former Rabbi at the Synagogue," she said. "They all wanted to see the Romans removed from Judea and for God to be elevated to His rightful position as their King instead of some emperor in Rome who was idolatrous and who even considered himself a god."

Simeon listened intently. These were exactly the kind of things he wanted to know.

Miriam continued, "The more their group huddled together, the more they became convinced they needed to take action to hasten the coming of God's Messia--the Anointed One-- who would become the real King of the Jews. Herod the Great died around the time of your birth about 10 years ago, but that false ruler was despised by all serious Jews."

"What happened after he died?" Simeon asked.

"Well, his kingdom was divided among his three living sons. He had killed several of his other sons thinking they were plotting to take away his throne." Miriam sighed. "Can you imagine, a father killing his own sons because he suspected them of treason, when it wasn't true? How crazy was that? Now his second son, Herod Antipas, rules over the region of the Galilee."

"Oh, I've heard of him, Mother" said Simeon. "All of my friends believe he is a terrible king. So do I."

Miriam answered, "Yes, he's a tyrant, but he's not actually a king. When his father divided up the kingdom just prior to his death, each of his three sons received a portion of the land to rule. The Romans would not let any of them be officially called a king, so Herod Antipas is actually called the Tetrarch of Galilee, which is not as powerful as a king. I know, many of the Galileans refer to Antipas as the King, but he really is just like a governor over the area."

"Oh, I'll be sure to explain that to my friends. He's not so important! But what happened to Abba?"

"Well," Miriam began, "The Roman Emperor, Augustus Caesar, issued a decree for the second census of this area around the time you were eight years old. This method of counting people in order to tax them more was just too much to take. Judas of Galilee, your father, and other zealous men became even more convinced they had to do something about the wickedness polluting our country. These Romans had to be removed so God could rule. Judas rallied all of the men and challenged them to arm for a battle. Most of the men were farmers, fishermen, and shepherd. Not soldiers. They had very few weapons, and most of those were feeble, so they didn't feel adequate to fight against the trained soldiers in the Roman army.

Hundreds of soldiers resided in Sepphoris, but they also had a large armory there that was relatively unguarded. The Romans didn't think anyone was actually going to try and rob the armory right under their noses. But that's the plan Judas proposed."

"You mean, they all planned to attack the Romans without weapons? How could they possibly win against the soldiers?"

"They decided to use clever strategies to gain victory rather than sheer force. Since your father and other craftsmen had made friends with some of the Romans, Judas proposed they infiltrate the headquarters in the city and move around casually as if they were just working there. When everybody was set in place a signal would be given to alert the men outside the city that it was time to sneak into the area of the armory. Your father, Judas, our Rabbi, and a few other loyal men were the main ones who were inside and could provide access to the others through some obscure back gates to Sepphoris. These entry points were seldom guarded, and they weren't being protected the night the plot was launched."

"Wasn't that a dangerous plan, mother? What if something went wrong or they were discovered? Weren't they stealing the weapons and wouldn't the Romans be furious?"

Miriam replied, "Your father and the others signaled the men, got them inside the garrison, and quietly gained access to the armory. The zealots grabbed as many weapons as they could and tried to escape. Unfortunately, some Roman guards heard the noise of clacking metal and found your father's group trying to steal the weapons. When the alarm was sounded to the rest of the army, only a very small group was able to getaway. Eleazar the Rabbi and several other insurgents were killed during the resulting skirmish. However, no Romans died in the conflict."

Simeon watched his mother grow emotional, but stayed silent.

After what seemed to be several minutes but was actually less than one, Miriam added, "Really, it was a blessing that your father died in the battle because Judas and others were captured, tortured, humiliated, and ultimately crucified because of their audacious attempt to rob the armory. Those who were arrested and martyred also learned prior to their deaths that the Romans aggressively persecuted the families of those who were judged. Perhaps because your father was liked by many of the Romans, the soldiers never came after me or the rest of our family."

"Yes, Mother, I understand."

She continued, "I feared for many months following your father's death. Eleazar and the others were buried by the Romans in a mass grave outside of Sepphoris. I only know the general area of the burial, but I'm afraid to visit because I'm concerned the Roman soldiers would deal harshly with me just for coming to the spot. I've never been able to honor your father's burial place until this day."

"Oh, mother, I'm so sorry that my father died in such a terrible way. But I believe he died a hero trying to honor God! I'm proud of his desire to be free and wanting to make us safe and secure from the invaders of our homeland. I hate the Romans," Simeon said, as he crossed his arms. "And I know why he felt he had to resist them even if it cost him his life."

"Simeon," Miriam responded with tenderness. "We all miss your father and wish things were different but I, too, am proud of his desire to serve God, even though it cost him everything. I just want you to promise me you will never do anything so rash or hasty as trying to resist the Roman army like your father. I couldn't bear the thought of losing you, too." Miriam pulled her son into a tight hug. "You are my oldest son and I want you to stay with me, your brother, and sister and not fight against our oppressors and end up like your father. Please promise me you won't leave me!"

"Mother, I promise to stay with you and protect you as long as you live," Simeon replied. Little did he know that one day he would be plunged into a conflict not of his making, but one that would turn his entire world upside down.

He desperately wished his Abba was still around to teach him.

CHAPTER TWO

A Zealot is Recruited

SIMEON GREW IN strength, stature, and knowledge, turning into a fine and honorable young man. Miriam was so proud of her sons and daughter. Their life was still very hard and she lived with her parents, providing for their needs, as well as those of her children. They had some resources to help meet the physical needs of the family, which was a huge blessing.

Shortly before he turned nineteen years old, Simeon noticed a beautiful young girl from the neighboring village. Her name was Martha. She was less than a year younger than he was. She saw in Simeon a handsome and hard-working young man. She wept when he told her the story of his father, and she commiserated with him about trying to help meet the needs of his mother and siblings.

The Roman scourge continued in the country, and their rule was growing more oppressive. In Jerusalem, things had gone from bad to worse. When Herod the Great died, to the relief of most of the Jews, the issue of succession arose. Herod knew, in spite of his priceless remodeling of the Jewish Temple in Jerusalem, that most of the Jewish people never appreciated him. In his typical paranoid condition, and believing the Jews would actually rejoice at the news of his demise, he ordered that upon his death his soldiers were to gather up 100 prominent Jewish leaders and summarily execute them. Herod surmised, this was the only way the Jews would actually weep at the time of his death.

But the order was never carried out.

Herod left Jerusalem and Judea in the hands of his oldest living son, Archelaus. This man proved to be nearly as paranoid and ruthless as his father. In fact, Archelaus made the Roman government so angry with his poor management style, they removed him from office in 6 AD. At that point, the Romans installed a system of governance where Roman Prefects or Procurators ruled over the region.

The local people referred to them as Governors, but the supervision of the Jews was even worse. These Prefects were always Gentiles, and many of them came from Italy with little or no knowledge of the Jewish culture, condition or religion. They often worshipped their foreign gods, including Caesar, and this infuriated the monotheistic Jews--especially the budding Zealot Party, those who desired Theocracy.

Another issue with the Roman governors was they saw a minor province like Judea as a stepping stone to larger and more influential posts. Therefore, most of these Prefects attempted to gain wealth and status as rapidly as they could. They often saw these provinces as their own personal treasuries, so graft and corruption were the norm.

Some of the governors increased the tax burden on their subjects in order to pad their own purses. They hired Jewish tax collectors--called publicans--to gather taxes from the citizens. They did so with great vigor, because they were able to skim a hefty portion of the monies before passing their collections along to the Roman treasury.

These taxes were especially punitive for the Jewish people, who were already heavily weighed down by their own religious obligations, like the half-Shekel Temple Tax required from all Jewish adult males. The costs of providing multiple offerings as part of their routine sacrifices and feast days, have led many historians to conclude the Jewish people may have had the heaviest burden of taxation of any group within the entire Roman Empire.

Of course, Roman leaders were eager to benefit from this lucrative financial arrangement. During the time of the Procurator System, the governors would also accept bribes from various religious groups of the Jews so that they could gain favor and influence with the Romans. One such example emerged as an annual bribe for the governor from one of the leading religious parties within Judaism.

The Sadducees.

These aristocratic and wealthy Jews were powerful even though they were few in number. The Sadducees had primary control over the Jewish High Court known as the *Sanhedrin.* And they almost always controlled the High Priest's office because of their wealth and corruption. Every year they would pay a hefty indemnity to the Roman Prefect to secure one of their own in this highest of religious offices. With the Roman Governors approval, the High Priest Office would, once again, be secured by a member of the Sadducee Party.

Over time, the governance of Jerusalem and Judea devolved into a cesspool of graft, corruption, bribes, and influence peddling. The Roman Prefect system remained in place for several decades, adding even more bondage for the Jewish people who yearned ever-increasingly for deliverance. Back in Galilee, things were not quite so oppressive, although Herod Antipas had his own methods of enriching himself on the backs of his Jewish subjects.

Simeon and Martha were making plans for a betrothal period--but first, Simeon had to negotiate with Martha's father, Ephraim, about a dowry price. Normally, this would have been a transaction settled by the two fathers, but obviously, Eleazar had been martyred more than a decade earlier. Miriam was in complete agreement about Martha joining the family, but Ephraim had to approve. Simeon and Miriam met with Ephraim. Martha had regularly expressed her wishes to her father, but the final determination would have to come from him.

When they arrived at Ephraim's home, mother and son were invited to participate in the customary sharing of hospitality--some light food and water or milk. As they enjoyed the refreshments, they passed the time with casual conversation. But they all knew the real purpose for their visit.

Simeon mustered up his courage and began to speak, "Sir, I know you're aware that my father died many years ago so he's not here to ask you what I'm about to propose." He immediately regretted using the word, propose.

Ephraim interrupted, addressing both of his guests, "I knew Eleazar many years ago, and I want you both to know how much I admired him and his love for God and family. He did work for my family years ago and there was no better craftsman anywhere in Galilee. I'm so sorry you have had to endure these years of hardship because of his untimely death."

"We appreciate your kind words," Simon replied. "I was so young when Abba died, I always love hearing stories from those who knew him back then. Thank you for reminding us of his honorable work and noble life." Simeon took a deep breath and chose his next words carefully. "I've been working hard in the business my father founded as a stonemason. I've gained a significant amount of experience as an apprentice for your friend, Joel. And I'm sure you could ask him about my work ethic and accomplishment."

Ephraim hastily interjected, "I already have." His quick reply made everyone chuckle.

For a brief instant, Simeon felt a little more at ease as he continued his purposed presentation. "Sir, I come to you today because I want to humbly request that you allow me to marry your daughter whom I love very much."

For a moment--which seemed like an eternity to Simeon--there was no response from Ephraim. It was as if he was, once again, sizing up the young man.

Finally, the silence was broken when Martha, who had been hiding behind a curtain in another room, burst out with emotion, "Say, something Daddy!" The surprise of Martha's passionate interruption brought more than a chuckle. This time it was a hearty laugh.

When things settled down Ephraim began to speak. "Simeon, I believe you are a fine young man and I think you come from a great family." The pause allowed for

Simeon to believe there was a "but" coming. Sure enough, Ephraim continued, "But I have some questions I need to ask you before I give my decision. I know Eleazar died many years ago while participating in a plot to try and resist the Roman occupation of our country. That was such a tragedy. What do you think about your father's actions and his tragic death along with the other men who followed the doomed dreams of Judas the Galilean?"

Simeon pondered the significance of Ephraim's question. If he answered the wrong way and offended Martha's dad, he might not ever receive his blessing and lose Martha forever. But the more he thought about it he knew he had to be true to his own heart. His mind raced as he tried to remember any past conversations with Ephraim, any particular thing he might have said about the Roman occupation. In the heat of the moment, no clear thoughts came to him about which side of the issue to emphasize.

Slowly and deliberately, Simeon began to frame his response.

"Sir," Simeon pushed out the words, "I believe my father was a hero. He loved God and he loved his nation. He hated the oppressive boot of Rome. From what I remember of him, he taught us to love the One and only True God. We were not to have any other gods before Him. We were not to entertain any idols," he said, beginning to raise his voice. "We were to never take the Name of the Lord our God in vain. These were some things my father taught me. Oh, how I wish he could have taught me more!" He caught himself and calmed his voice a bit. " But Sir, I loved my father, and I hate what the Romans did to him, to my mother, and to my family. They are terrible, wicked, godless, enemies of our nation and our God. If it were in my power I would love to see all of them eradicated from the face of the earth. Like my father, I feel I must resist the pagan rot of Roman imperialism. They will completely destroy our nation and our religion if they have a chance to do so."

Ephraim listened, impressed with tthe young man's passionate monologue.

Simeon continued, "As my father joined with some other patriotic zealots, I believe it might be incumbent upon me to make similar sacrifices to protect my God, my nation, my mother, and my own family. I'm not sure, Sir, that's what you want to hear, but that's what's passionately in my heart and I must be true to God and to myself. I love your daughter. I want to marry her. And I hope with all my heart that my response to your questions hasn't jeopardized that."

In the background, Martha was quietly crying, unsure if that was the response her father wanted to hear. Had Simeon's passionate answer to her father ruined their chances of a future together? Was her dad horrified by Simeon's words? Martha patiently waited for someone to break the awkward silence.

Then she saw that her father was about to speak.

"Simeon," Ephraim measured his response, "I wasn't sure about your position on some of these issues, and I was afraid you were not worthy of my daughter if you held to the wrong opinion. I wanted you to explain to me your thoughts about your father because I knew that would reveal the true attitude of your heart. I appreciate your honesty, even though you were uncertain about my position on these matters." There was an uncomfortable pause before Ephraim continued his assessment of this young man's status. "Therefore, I have made a decision." Everyone in the room waited in absolute silence. A rooster crowed in the distance. Ephraim's usual joyful countenance seemed subdued, even anxious. He took a deep breath as he prepared to render his verdict.

"Simeon," another deep breath, "I'm so pleased to hear your response about these Roman tyrants. I always admired your father because of his deep conviction about these matters. I was even more impressed when I heard he had given his highest sacrifice to try and liberate us. I was hoping that maybe you had inherited the same attitude, the same passion, and the same willingness to stand up against these heathen invaders. Simeon, it would be my honor to have you marry my Martha. I now know you will provide for her and protect her with the same love and energy that I have tried to give her all of her life."

A collective sigh was audible to everyone in the room, resulting even in some noticeable snickers. Ephraim continued, "I have discussed this matter with Martha's mother, and because you are just now coming to a point of proficiency in your masonry work, and because you have been trying to help out with your mother and family since your father died, we want to release you from having to pay a dowry for Martha to become your wife. You can marry her soon and take her to your home."

He then looked over at his daughter and asked, "Is that acceptable to you Martha?"

She tried to verbalize an answer, but all that came out was a muffled sound of air mixed with a stream of tears. Her exaggerated nodding of yes with her head was clear for everyone to see and interpret. Especially, Simeon. He, too, began to feel tears running down his cheeks.

Ephraim broke the tension of the emotional moment and began to speak again. "Simeon, rather than pay a dowry, one day I may call on you to do a special project for me. When I redeem that promise, I hope you will respond with unhesitating affirmation and do what I ask of you."

"Absolutely," answered Simeon, "I'll be happy to help you any way that I can. And thank you for allowing me to have my wife that I will love for as long as I live!"

At that moment, a voice called to Ephraim from beyond the door. Ephraim excitedly opened the door for another visitor. "Simeon, let me introduce to you my cousin who will also be so glad you will be part of the family." Turning to his new guest Ephraim explained, "We all just agreed that Simeon and Martha will be getting married soon."

"Hallelujah," was the cousin's heartfelt response. "It will be great to have you as part of our amazing family," he said.

"How rude of me" said Ephraim. "Simeon, meet your soon cousin-to-be, this is my Uncle's son, Jesus Barabbas--but we all just call him Barabbas."

CHAPTER THREE

A Zealot is Energized

ABOUT SIX MONTHS into the betrothal period, Ephraim, his wife, and Miriam decided it was time for Simeon and Martha to be wed. Since there was no dowry price to be paid, Simeon did not need to keep working on that issue. He had been diligently working on the place where they would live. About eight years after Eleazar's martyrdom, both of Miriam's parents also died. Because she was an only child, she inherited their home. An accomplished carpenter and stonemason, Simeon had been working for months leading up to their wedding, adding a beautiful addition to the house so that he and his new bride would have their own sequestered quarters in the family home.

They wound up having one of the nicer places in the city of Cana and Simeon was eager to welcome his bride to their first dwelling. A short time later, they were married and Simeon took Martha into their home.

And a new chapter in their life began.

A few years later, God blessed the happy couple with a little, baby boy. They agreed to name him, Eleazar. Even Ephraim applauded that decision. Within several years, they saw a daughter named Lydia and another son named John born into their family. Miriam was ecstatic to have little grandchildren running around, especially since her other two children were also grown and married. They didn't live very far away, but so far they had no children. When they eventually had kids, Miriam thought they should move closer to her.

Such were the dreams of a grandmother.

Meanwhile, Simeon's work had become famous in the city. He was every bit the stonemason and carpenter that his father had been, and then some, even eclipsing Eleazar's reputation in Galilee.

Because of his skill, Simeon had been contracted to work on several major building projects in the area. The Tetrarch of Galilee, Herod Antipas, hired him for several important assignments at his palace. When other building opportunities developed along the shores of the Sea of Galilee, Simeon got the jobs on the referral of Antipas.

Simeon had also been hired to do work in Nazareth.

On one occasion, he was taken to Sepphoris for some contract labor. It was surreal for Simeon to be at the Roman garrison where his father had been killed while fighting. While there, he learned where the mass grave was--the one where his father had been buried.

Several evenings, he found himself looking pensively in the direction of the burial site, doing all he could to keep his emotions from boiling over with hatred for these Roman occupiers. As he kept his own identity closely guarded, he wondered if some of the soldiers there now were a part of what happened that night many years earlier when his father was killed.

Simeon's interest in the anti-Roman movement continued to grow, fueled by his cousin Barabbas, who was now leading the burgeoning Zealot movement.

He and Barabbas were just casual friends at the beginning of his marriage to Martha. They would see each other only once or twice a year. But now, after more than ten years, Simeon found himself hanging out with Barabbas more frequently. A group of patriots had gravitated Barabbas, and the movement seemed to be growing stronger--and more agitated-- toward their Roman oppressors.

Each of these Zealots had a story to tell about Roman atrocities and murders that had impacted their family. Simeon was certainly eager to tell the story of his martyred father. One kindred spirit, a man named Micah, spoke of an unimaginable tragedy regarding his family.

Two years earlier, his father had been walking down a path in a place called the Valley of the Doves between Tiberias and Nazareth, when, to his horror, he came upon two dead Roman soldiers. They had been stabbed by spears. It appeared they had been recently ambushed--the bodies were still warm. Nothing had been taken. It was as if the attackers had fled immediately. Perhaps it was the noise of his father approaching that hastened their exit.

As Micah's father stared in disbelief at the scene before him, he suddenly heard noises and voices and he spun around. He was confronted by roughly ten Roman soldiers who glared at him as if he had been the perpetrator. They jumped on his father, viciously beating him.

Despite his vehement declaration of innocence--even pointing out that he didn't have a drop of blood on himself except his own--the Roman soldiers apprehended him and hauled him and the dead bodies off to Sepphoris. There, they presented the circumstantial case against Micah's father, that they found him standing over the bodies. The Roman soldiers, filled with rage, again beat and kicked his father. As they pummeled him, they demanded to know where he lived. He weakly said he lived in Magdala near Tiberias.

Micah then told us they crucified his father outside the fortress of Sepphoris--the same place where Simeon's father had been executed. Still hot with rage that a Jew dared kill two Romans, a group of soldiers headed to Magdala to find Micah's family. Micah was away visiting relatives near Jericho when the Romans stormed his family's home. Others in the city described the scene as it unfolded. The soldiers were in a blind rage. They dragged Micah's mother, two young sisters, and his grandparents out of the house and then burned it to the ground. The Romans screamed out the charges against Micah's father and boasted about how they had brutally crucified him.

Now, because of his supposed atrocity, they would pay with *their* lives. Immediately, and mercilessly, the soldiers slashed and viciously stabbed Micah's mother, sisters, and grandparents. Villagers watched helplessly as they died.

But the Romans never knew they had missed one of the family members--Micah.

When he returned back to Magdala, Micah's whole world was shattered by what happened to his entire family. Soon, the young man was fully committed to the cause of resisting the Romans, even to the point of his own death, if necessary. He hated the Romans and wanted to exact vengeance upon them in any way possible.

Becoming a Zealot provided the best way to fight back.

Micah's story was among the more horrific accounts shared among the followers of Barabbas, but almost everyone had a similar story about Roman brutality and atrocity. Their hatred and bitterness reached a boiling point and they were determined that something had to be done. Upon hearing about Micah's testimony, Simeon realized how similar his experience was with Micah's. He began to shake as he pondered how close his own family had come to a similar fate at the time of his father's death.

But God had spared him, and Simeon was convinced it was because God wanted him to join the cause of trying to liberate Judea from Roman bondage, thus helping usher in the Messianic Kingdom. He became committed than ever to the cause of Judean liberty and Theocracy. Martha was totally supportive of her husband's zealous ambitions, although there was always dissonance because of the evil atrocities of the Romans. She feared that one day Simeon might experience their wrath.

The fledgling Zealot Party was a reaction to Roman dominance and brutality. The Sadducees were the most wealthy and powerful Jewish political party of the day. They controlled the High Priesthood and the Sanhedrin. Although they were not numerous, they had political clout with the Romans and walked a fine line between their religion and the pragmatic compromises with the Prefect needed to maintain a precarious peace.

The Pharisees, however, were the most *popular* religious sect of Judaism. Most of the Jewish people looked to the Pharisees for genuine spiritual leadership. This, even though their doctrine was very connected to the Mosaic Law and they had added so many traditions to it, things that became a huge burden on the people.

A third sect of Judaism was known as the Essenes. Members of this group chose sequestered and monastic lives, primarlily in the Judean wilderness. They believed-- at least philosophically--much like the Pharisees, but they felt the religious leaders in Jerusalem had distorted true worship, turning Temple worship into an opportunity for merchandising. So, they stopped participating in Temple worship and observances. They cultivated their own solemn rituals, but were also known for several unique practices. The Essenes lived communally, holding all things in common. And they worked painstakingly to make copies of the Hebrew Scriptures.

In fact, the Essenes hid many of their valuable treasures--sacred scrolls of Hebrew writings--which were discovered two-thousand years later in caves around the region of their main community, Qumran, near the Dead Sea.

According to the Jewish historian Flavius Josephus, the Fourth Philosophical School of the Jewish religion was a group called the Zealots. Josephus was a General of the Jewish Army during the Jewish Revolt of 66 AD. He agreed to leave his post as a General and began working for the Romans, documenting the events of Jewish history--including the Great Revolt.

Josephus reserved his harshest criticism for the Zealots. He called them bandits and robbers and laid the fault of Jerusalem's fall and the Temple's destruction by the Romans, squarely at their feet. But it was to this nationalistic party that Simeon and his compatriots were prepared to give their lives.

In Galilee, the Zealot movement was gaining momentum, and people were regularly gravitating to their cause. Most Zealots maintained normal jobs and had strong families. They were active in their Synagogues and gave alms regularly to assist with the needs of the poor. Simeon did more than most when it came to supporting widows and their children. Having grown up with so little and knowing the challenges his mother faced without a husband to help at home, Simeon and Martha were quick to respond to people in similar situations. Since God had blessed Simeon's business and he had some extra money to allocate to benevolent causes, he was always looking to be a blessing to those in need.

One family that lived fairly close to Cana particularly tugged at his heart. Simeon was working there, near his in-laws home, when he met a young man, just barely old enough to have achieved his Bar Mitzvah, and he was the only son of a widow. Simeon started talking to the boy and he immediately felt a connection.

Simeon asked him, "What happened to your father, and how old were you when he died?"

The boy's name was Philip and he began telling his story, "I was eight-years-old when my father was taken."

"What do you mean taken?" said Simeon.

"The Roman soldiers came and dragged him away, right in front of me and my mother. They were yelling and screaming that he had been involved in a robbery at one of their check- points and that he had stolen some weapons. My mother pleaded with them. She swore to them my father was at home when the alleged theft took place. But they did not believe her. My dad matched a rough description a Roman guard had provided, but that was good enough for the soldiers to conclude my father was guilty. They were beating him right in our yard, and then they put him in a wagon and hauled him away."

"What happened to him?" asked Simeon.

"We didn't find anything out for several weeks, but one of our neighbors who had business in Nazareth finally returned home. He had traveled the short distance up to Sepphoris and inquired about my father. He was told my father had resisted their interrogation and during a struggle had died. Our neighbor asked for some personal items that might confirm it was my father, and they gave him a ring."

"Did your mother recognize it?

"Yes," Philip replied. "As soon as my mother saw it she collapsed to the floor. The Romans told our neighbor the dead Jew had been buried in a mass grave outside Sepphoris. My mother gave me the ring."

Philip proudly showed the ring to Simeon.

When Simeon heard the story, his heart ached. Philip was almost the same age he was when his Abba was killed. And that also happened at Sepphoris, and it was also due to a robbery-- of weapons. The mention of a mass grave outside the city also hit a nerve. Unlike his father, Philip's father really did appear to be innocent. Philip's mother

Lois dogmatically declared her husband was at home at the time of the alleged robbery. Apparently, that didn't matter to the capricious Roman soldiers who were just looking for a scapegoat.

Simeon discovered that Philip and his mother had very little and barely eked out a living. Often times, Philip had been forced to beg just to get food. Simeon regularly stopped by Philip's house to make sure he and his mother had food and other necessities. He even used his carpentry skills to fix things around their home, things that had fallen into disrepair.

Martha knew the family and came over from time to time to help Lois around the house. Both Simeon and Martha were gratified to be able to provide for some of the needs for this desperate family. Over time, Martha and Lois became quite close.

And they shared a growing disdain for the Roman butchers.

CHAPTER FOUR

A Zealot is Challenged

SIMEON TOOK HIS family to Jerusalem several times a year to observe special feast days and offer the Passover sacrifice in the month of Nisan. He wanted his children to experience what he had missed growing up as an adolescent without a father to take him to the Temple. He had a hazy memory of the few times he went with his Abba as a child--it was always a special experience. Simeon wanted his children to have an unforgettable memory of going to the Temple of God and worshipping Him through the Jewish customs.

With each trip to Jerusalem, however, Simeon became more and more disenchanted with the religious leaders and their cozy relationship with the Roman elites.

The activities at the Temple courtyard had turned into a bazaar, with things being sold and sacrifices being auctioned for offerings. Money-changers were everywhere and the reverence and holiness of the Temple compound had been defiled and distorted into a marketplace.

These things must not have pleased God.

Still, Simeon and his family tried to have the full spiritual experience of making sincere offerings to God at His Temple. But it seemed more and more likely that someday he might have to offer *himself* in order to right the wrongs of the escalating Roman oppression.

He actually came close one time to the Roman Governor during those year--a man named Pontius Pilate. Simeon and his family were near the Temple complex after offering their Passover lamb, when a Roman entourage passed by on their way to the fortress of Antonia, just northwest of the Temple. In the parade were many Roman soldiers. Their primary responsibility was to guard the Prefect. On that particular occasion, Pontius Pilate impulsively ordered the processional to stop several hundred cubits from the entrance to Antonia. He dismounted his horse and started to mingle with his Jewish subjects, to the horror and dismay of his troops.

Several of the soldiers quickly moved to get between Pilate and the citizens. But Pilate seemed undeterred, and he started walking up to people, shaking hands, and sharing pleasantries. Pilate had to know what the soldiers knew, that Jewish Zealots were often active in the crowds, even committing assassinations upon unsuspecting Romans and Roman sympathizers. One extremely hostile branch of the Zealots even assumed the title *Sicarii* because of their unorthodox and brutal practices. A small Roman sword--more like a dagger--was called in Latin, a *Sica* and was used for close combat situations.

This group of proactive Zealots took the name *Sicarii* because they would blend into a crowd with their flowing robes while hiding a *Sica* under their garments. When they approached an unsuspecting Roman, or a Jew who was a Roman sympathizer, they would move in close and stab the target in the ribs near the heart. Even as the victim was falling to the ground, the assassin would slip quietly into the press of people and nonchalantly escape.

The *Sicarii* became more emboldened over the years and reports about murders of Roman officials escalated. So when Pilate plunged into the crowd, the soldiers understandably panicked as they feared some *Sicarii* might attempt to commit the ultimate assassination, of the highest-ranking Roman in the nation.

It was on this occasion that Pilate actually walked up to Simeon, extending his hand as a gesture of friendship. He also rubbed the heads of his two sons. Then as quickly as it happened, Pilate moved on by greeting other Jewish people along the way. Simeon thought at that moment how easy it would have been to eliminate the most powerful Roman in the country.

But not that day.

Back in Galilee, the Zealots were growing stronger, and it seemed like people were talking more and more about them doing something to show the Romans that God was still working. But another phenomenon was also being discussed around the area. There were rumors about a man who seemed to speak remarkable things about God.

Everyone was talking about this man from Nazareth.

Simeon first heard about him was from Martha. On one of Simeon's rare business trips to Tiberias--to help build a government building--he was away from his family for three days. Tiberias was an important Roman city in Galilee, but it wasn't a military installation. There were various cities like it in the region. In fact, there were Ten Roman Cities south of Tiberias, some on each side of the Jordan River, known as the Decapolis. Beth Shean was one of the most glorious of these Roman-styled cities of the Decapolis, with colonnade lined streets on the Cardo (the main road through the heart of the city), an amphitheater, a hippodrome for chariot races, a bath-house, and many other Roman-styled features that made the many displaced Romans feel more at home. All Decapolis cities were built with a very similar architecture.

Tiberias, however, was a little different, which is why it wasn't considered part of the Decapolis. This city had been built by the son of Herod the Great. Herod Antipas, the Tetrarch of Galilee, had an ambitious desire to build this resort city on the shores of the Sea of Galilee, also known as the Lake of Gennesaret. Trying to establish himself as a great builder in his own right, Antipas had decided to impress the Emperor of Rome and build a city and unashamedly name it after him--Tiberias.

Augustus Caesar had died in 14 AD, and he was succeeded by Tiberias. That is when Herod Antipas laid the foundation for a new city over the meager buildings that existed at the site. Ever trying to improve the city he hoped one day would welcome the sitting Emperor, Antipas kept building bigger and nicer palaces and homes where the Romans could reside or visit. That is why Simeon was contracted to work there.

Once, again, Antipas recognized Simeon's skills and paid him handsomely to come over and contribute to his burgeoning masterpiece for the Emperor. These carpentry opportunities, were lucrative and brought Simeon into increased contact with Romans, even if there were only a few soldiers around. Still, every encounter caused him anxiety as his smoldering hatred for the Gentiles was fueled with each passing week. His downtime in Tiberias gave him plenty of time to think about the best way he and his Zealot friends could one day cripple the growing presence of Roman paganism.

It was while Simeon was on this business trip that the most remarkable thing happened in Cana. The children were now old enough to stay home by themselves for a short time. Eleazar was growing into a young man who could watch over his siblings, so Martha ventured out on a very rare, solo excursion. Most Jewish women seldom left their homes for a social event unchaperoned by their husbands, but Martha and Simeon had been invited to a special occasion.

In his absence, Martha decided to go alone to the marriage celebration of the year.

Well, she wasn't really alone. Lois, her widow friend from nearby, came over to attend the wedding ceremony, as well. They thought it would be fun. Cana's most significant leader, Caleb, was hosting a wedding for his only son, Mattathias. The groom was marrying one of the most beautiful young girls in the area, the daughter of another civic leader, Aaron. The bride's name was Sarah. This big event was actually the final evening of the ceremony that would unite these two noble families in the area. Everything was perfect as the celebration churned on and it truly was amazing how many people were there for the occasion.

In fact, it seemed like Caleb was getting just a little distressed as the evening progressed. Unbeknown to most of the guests, the host was watching as the supply of wine he had purchased for the party was rapidly dwindling. It would be a terrible act of inhospitality if the fruit of the vine ran out before the guests did. Actually, some people were starting to drift away from the celebration, but Martha and Lois were enjoying every part of the festivities which seldom occurred in their quiet village.

Suddenly, there was a scurry of activity as Caleb beckoned to some of his household servants. Mattathias and Sarah were completely immersed in mingling with their friends and guests and did not notice what was taking place. They were were both in a position, however, to see what was unfolding. It had happened. The wine had run out and Caleb was scrambling to cover it up.

Some visitors, people Martha didn't recognize, were standing near Caleb. There was a lovely woman speaking to Caleb, who then she made a hasty trek across the courtyard to a handsome young man, about Simeon's age. They were engaged in an intense conversation. The young man seemed to have an entourage. A few animated gestures later, the woman motioned for some servants to come over. Unable to hear what they were saying, Martha and Lois watched with keen interest as a drama unfolded before them. The waiters went over to the young man and it appeared that he gave them some instructions. They rushed off, presumably to follow his   directives.

Soon, the servants returned, laboring under the weight of heavy stone water pots, the kind usually reserved for ceremonial washing. There were six of them and they were empty. By now, Martha and Lois had moved closer to the action. Caleb was addressing another issue in the courtyard but still seemed intent on resolving the wine issue.

Martha and Lois could hear a little of what was going on. The young man had told the servants to fill the pots with water to the very brim. What was happening the women wondered? The man then said to the servants,

"You have done well. Now, draw some of the liquid out of one of the water pots and take it to the governor of the feast."

They did exactly as instructed. When Caleb tasted the water, he immediately reacted and called Mattathias over, making him taste the water. It was then offered to Sarah's father, Aaron. They were astonished at what they were drinking.

The water was now wine.

Caleb had managed to keep the disaster from Aaron about running out of wine, so this development solicited a remarkable comment from Aaron, "Most of the time the new wine is brought out first, and later in the evening the less flavorful wine is distributed and usually no one notices. But you have kept the best wine until now. This is the best wine I've ever tasted. Where did you find it?"

Caleb didn't exactly know what had happened. He queried one of his servants, who said, "This man, the son of the woman you were talking to earlier, had us fill all these pots with water. Then, somehow, he turned all of those pots full of water, into pots full of new wine." He enthusiastically added, "It was a miracle!"

Martha and Lois stared at each other in disbelief.

They moved over to the water pots and sampled the contents themselves. Indeed, it was the best tasting wine they had ever savored. Needless to say, they had to know the identity of this miracle man. But he and his entourage had already left the celebration, so Martha had to do some sleuthing.

She boldly walked up to the woman who had earlier been addressing Caleb and introduced herself. "Hi, my name is Martha, and this is my friend Lois. We noticed you from a distance and didn't recognize you as being from Cana."

"My name is Mary," she responded, "I'm from Nazareth. Our family has known Caleb and Mattathias for many years. We were excited to come for the wedding celebration of Mattathias and Sarah."

Martha cleverly asked, "You said, *we* were excited to come. Who is with you?"

Mary unhesitatingly said, "I came with my daughters to see the wedding, so they could get some ideas for the future and their weddings. And a few other friends came over from Nazareth with us."

Lois spoke up, "Did your husband come?"

"No. My husband Joseph died several years ago, so it's just me and the children now," Mary answered.

Martha interjected, "I thought I saw you talking to a young man who had some other fellows with him. Someone, you know?"

Mary, seemingly oblivious to the interrogation that was going on, said, "Oh that was my oldest son. His name is Jesus. He just recently left our home in Nazareth and has been traveling around with a group of men he has been teaching. They spend most of their time in Capernaum, but I was so glad we got to see each other here at the wedding. I wasn't sure he was coming, but I knew he had been invited."

Martha could hardly contain her excitement to ask the next question. "I don't want to seem forward, but Lois and I happened to observe what your son did when the wine ran out. We watched the servants fill the water pots as Jesus told them, and then he turned the water, into wine. How did he do that?"

Mary said, "I have no idea. I have always known that Jesus was a special gift from God and destined for greatness, but how he did such a miracle, I can't say. I've never seen anything like that myself. But after doing it, he quietly walked over to me, kissed me on the cheek, and told me he loved me. Then he simply led his friends out into the darkness. I was hoping he was going back to Nazareth with us for a few days, but apparently not."

Martha's enthusiasm could no longer be contained. "I can't believe what we witnessed," she said. "We tasted the wine, and it was the sweetest tasting drink I have ever put in my mouth. It was incredible what your Jesus did!"

"Oh, yes. You don't know the half of it," said Mary, laughingly. "But my guess is, you'll be hearing more about Jesus of Nazareth before too long."

"I hope so," said Lois. "I can't wait to tell my son Philip all about this chance encounter."

Mary retorted, "I'm not so sure it was just a chance encounter. Somehow, I think God had a plan for this rendezvous." Then Mary, obviously ready to move on, said, "You ladies be safe going home."

Martha quickly responded, "It was so nice meeting you, Mary. You also be careful going home. We hope to see you again."

"I hope so, too," said Mary, as she walked out of the party with her daughters and friends.

Martha and Lois couldn't stop talking about what they had witnessed that evening. They shared it with the kids when they got home. They thought it was the greatest story they had ever heard. Martha couldn't wait to tell Simeon about what happened as soon as he arrived home.

CHAPTER FIVE

A Zealot Leader

SIMEON HAD HARDLY got in the door two days later before he was swamped by Martha and the kids. They were all eager to be the ones to tell their father what mother had seen and heard. But Martha insisted she be the one to tell Simeon what had happened. After recounting all the details about the wedding miracle, details that had been seared into her memory, Martha took a deep breath, realizing that her passionate account of the water becoming wine must have sounded unbelievable to Simeon. After giving him a minute to soak it all in, she asked, "Well, what do you think?"

Unsure how he should respond, Simeon said, "That's an amazing story. But it's hard to believe."

"I know, I know," she said. "If *you* were telling *me*, I would probably think it was a fanciful story embellished with myths, if I hadn't seen it myself. Just ask Lois. She'll tell you the very same story."

"Oh, I believe you, Martha," Simeon said, with an assuring tone. "It's just taking me a moment to think it all through. I do have a few questions. Is it okay if I ask you to expand on a few things?"

"Sure, ask away," was her quick reply. It was almost as if she was eager to share more details. The children were hanging on every word, and so far, the story was identical to the other times she told it. This was so exciting, even hearing over and over again.

Simeon began, "You said this man who did the miracle was named Jesus, and he came from Nazareth?"

"That's right," Martha confirmed.

"He was about my age?"

"That's my guess, "

"What did you say was the name of this widow's deceased husband?" Simeon asked.

Martha thought for moment and then said, "Mary mentioned, in passing, that her husband had died a few years earlier. I'm pretty sure she said his name was *Joseph.*"

"Did she say what Joseph did for a living in Nazareth?" asked Simeon.

"No, I don't believe she did." Martha wondered, "Why?"

Simeon answered in a reflective tone, "Well, during my stone masonry apprenticeship with Joel, I remember working in Nazareth and even at Sepphoris, with a very good carpenter named Joseph. And he had a son named Jesus who was learning. I wonder if the ones I knew from before? There can't be that many carpenters and stonemasons in Nazareth named Joseph, with a sons named Jesus. It has to be them, don't you think?"

"Well, Mary didn't say what her husband's craft was, but it sure sounds like it might be them," Martha agreed.

"As I remember it, this young man--Jesus--was a very good carpenter in his own right." Simeon added. "We even had some brief visits and laughed together. If it's the same person, I remember thinking at the time that he was a remarkable young man."

Martha hastened to add, "I'll bet it's the same fellow. One question--Did he ever turn water into wine when you saw him?" They all laughed.

But all these stories made both Simeon and Martha wonder about this amazing series of events.

Meanwhile, unbeknownst to Simeon, Barabbas and a few of his followers had moved into action against a small Roman scouting group near Gideon's Spring, south and east of Nazareth. This was the traditional place where Gideon had lead his ten thousand soldiers to get a drink of water. Based on God's directions to Gideon, he was to observe how the men drank their water from the spring. Those that just fell down and started hastily drinking the water with no concern for their surroundings or possible threats, were rejected from serving. Those few men, who carefully scooped up water in their hands and drank, all the while remaining vigilant for danger, were the ones God selected for service. Those few men totaled three hundred and they were about to fight a group of Midianites and Amalekites that numbered in the tens of thousands. In a miraculous moment of deliverance, God allowed Gideon to win a dynamic victory over their enemies.

There were five Roman soldiers in the small scouting group and they were oblivious to the past Jewish events at this spring. They had taken some time for leisure and refreshment. Ironically, they all shed their weapons in order to bathe and enjoy a moment of respite from their duties. As they were unaware of the dangers around them, the Zealots were able to quickly move toward the unwitting soldiers. The Roman fighters tried to make it to their weapons, but they were intercepted and massacred. The Zealot cause had, once again, become bloody with this attack on the enemy. On this day, everything changed as their tactics became much more proactive.

And the Roman response would be predictable.

This was not the first time Barabbas had shed Roman blood. A few years earlier he had secured some Roman iron-spears and ambushed two Roman soldiers along a path heading to Nazareth. As he made his undetected escape, one of their Jewish brothers had been arrested and later crucified by the Romans who found him near the dead soldiers.

That was Micah's father.

That false accusation led to the massacre of the rest of Micah's family in Magdala. Even though Micah was a fellow Zealot and close confidant, Barabbas never revealed his involvement in that episode. And he never planned to tell him.

Following the Gideon's Springs entrapment, the Galilean Zealots became bolder. Shortly after the attack, Barabbas gathered his group and started outlining a plan of action against the Roman scourge. Most members of the group were surprised to hear Barabbas bragging about having led the attack on the unsuspecting Romans. Although everyone in the region had heard about the massacre, only a few had concluded it was Barabbas and his friends. Even Simeon, who was attending this meeting, was shocked to hear the boasts. A wave of fear flooded Simeon's heart.

Things were escalating.

Barabbas spelled out his strategy. "Many years ago, one of our forefathers, Judas the Galilean, managed to embolden other Jewish Patriots to begin the liberation of our nation from Roman domination," Barabbas began. Just hearing the name--Judas the Galilean--made Simeon wince in pain. That's who had orchestrated the disaster at Sepphoris that resulted in his father's execution.

Barabbas continued, "In the spirit of those early Zealots, we are now prepared to rise up and strike a blow against Roman imperialism and set our nation on a course toward independence, freedom, and the re-establishment of the Davidic Monarchy, which was the golden age of our Jewish heritage."

The freedom-fighters voiced their agreement-- "Amen!"

Barabbas continued, "After our recent strike on the heathens at Gideon Springs, we must prepare for Roman reprisals. First, no one outside this room must mention a word about that attack and our involvement. The cruel Romans would kill all of us and our families if they discovered we were involved." That comment sent shivers down Simeon's spine. Could something happen to his family similar to the story Micah of Magdala that was told them so many months ago? Simeon agreed, this information could never get out.

Barabbas added, "We must be very careful who we let into our group too. If someone who is too weak or too uncommitted joined our ranks, they might be coerced to expose us, and that would be disastrous. So we must thoughtfully and strategically vet any person who would like to become a member of our Zealot assembly. We cannot make any mistakes."

Someone in the crowd spoke up and asked a question. "Barabbas, I've noticed that a couple of our brothers have left our group to follow someone else. What happened to them?"

Barabbas anticipated the question, but had hoped it would not be raised in public. However, since it was, he framed his answer carefully. "Well, that is true, but I want to reassure you that those men are not a threat to us--and they would never expose us. That being said, two of our own, Simon, known as the Zealot, and Judas the Iscariot have left us to follow after an emerging Rabbi who usually resides down in Capernaum. Apparently, they got religious and decided to follow him." There was a muffled laugh.

Then someone asked a follow-up question.

"But I thought those brothers were among our more committed members. In fact, Simon the Zealot took that name to boldly identify with our movement. And Judas went by the sobriquet, 'Iscariot' (which was a Hebrew iteration of the Latin, "Sicarii") because it implied he sympathized with that branch of our more radical members. How could both of those passionate soldiers abandon us to follow a religious seer?"

Barabbas, wanting to shut down this line of questioning, answered abruptly, "I don't know why they left us! They must have had their reasons, but apparently they thought this teacher named Jesus might be a revolutionary in his own right. They believed he was going to be able to set up a Kingdom and defeat the Romans. So they decided to follow him. More power to them."

"From Nazareth--can any good thing come from that place?" came a question from the back.

"Hey, I'm from Nazareth," someone else retorted.

Barabbas smiled and said, "See, I rest my case!"

Everyone got a momentary relief of laughter from the exchange. In reality, Barabbas was a little uneasy about how those brothers had abandoned him to follow this so-called, 'Prophet.' "We'll see who really makes a difference in the world?" Barabbas thought.

Chapter Six

A Zealot Rebellion

RUMORS OF THE mysterious Jewish Rabbi continued to circulate around the area. People everywhere seemed to be talking about his fascinating teachings and the amazing deeds he was performing. Testimonies from people, eyewitness accounts of divine wonders, were being shared all around Cana.

Some claimed they had been in a huge crowd near the Sea of Galilee when Jesus commanded them to all sit down on the ground. Then, as they watched, he lifted up a few small barley loaves and a couple of small fish, prayed to God, and proceeded to feed the entire crowd. They all ate until they were completely full, and then leftovers were gathered up--twelve large baskets full. One person reported that there were more than 5,000 men plus many women and children who ate that day.

"Unbelievable," was the most common response from those hearing the stories.

A friend of Simeon's and Martha's saw Jesus in Capernaum and told them personally how Jesus had healed a blind man, giving him his sight. The man had been blind his whole life, but Jesus made him see. They looked at each other with awe. Martha was quick to remind everyone of her personal experience with Jesus turning the water into wine. She had been there. She had seen it happen.

Almost everyone in Cana had been talking about that one for months.

Everyone in Galilee was curious about what this Jesus of Nazareth was all about. Martha, in particular, interested in finding out more about him. There was something so remarkably different about him and his captivating ways. In her heart, she just knew she had to find out who he really was and his significance to the Jewish people. For so long the Jewish nation had been expecting the coming of their Messiah, the 'Anointed One' and King. Was it possible that Jesus was this long-awaited Messiah?

Martha was determined to discover the truth.

The Roman troops were on high alert in Judea after the massacre at Gideon Springs had claimed five of their own. How dare these rebel Jews to challenge the might and authority of the legendary Roman war machine? Besides that incident in Galilee, there were reports of other atrocities being perpetrated in southern Judea around Jerusalem. Apparently, some members of the terrorist side of the Zealot Party, the Sicarii, had made some daring strikes on Romans, as well as some Jews who were cozy with the Romans.

During the Feast of Yom Kippur, the Day of Atonement in Jerusalem, the crowds had swelled and the mood was festive. On Yom Kippur, the High Priest would offer the sacrifice of a spotless lamb and take some of its blood into the Holy of Holies, or the "Holiest," inside the Temple. He would then sprinkle the blood on the mercy seat of the special altar to atone for the sins of the all the Jewish people for another year. By this blood of the lamb, the sins of the people would be symbolically covered.

The High Priest would also take some of the lamb's blood and put it on a male goat. This signified the placing of all the sins of the nation on that animal. Then this *Scapegoat* would be taken into the wilderness and released, never to return, as a picture of all the sins of the nation being taken away and forgotten. The wrath of God would be satisfied one more year because of the sacrifice of the lamb, and the removal of all the sins that were placed on the Scapegoat.

While Yom Kippur was being observed, a substantial contingent of the Roman Army had accompanied Pontius Pilate from Caesarea Marittima, where the Roman military quartered most of their soldiers during downtimes, over to Jerusalem just to keep a watch over the potentially volatile situation. These soldiers would garrison at the Fortress of Antonia, right next to the Temple. Near the large Temple complex that Herod the Great had extended and beautified, there was a huge number of pilgrims from around the region. They were there to offer sacrifices to God and to give their own offerings as well.

As Jewish dignitaries mingled with the crowd, the Roman Army had a substantial presence as a deterrent against possible violence. In the Court of the Gentiles, there were Rabbis with their students using the day for instruction and memorization.

Suddenly, as a trumpet sounded near the Temple Treasury indicating there were those giving offerings, there was a flurry of activity. The trumpet blast had apparently been a predetermined signal and several members of the "Sicarii" blazed into action. All around the courtyard, individuals who had been singled out for attack found themselves elbow to elbow with someone they didn't know. A thrust of the "Sica" made its way under the fifth rib of each victim. The wounded slumped to the ground and the assassins easily blended into the crowd and made a hasty retreat from the Temple complex. Fearing the Romans might close off all exits, it was mandatory that they get away as stealthily as possible.

One Roman soldier had drifted away from his cohort, helping a young child back to his parents. But this act of kindness was met with a piercing jab through the seam of his armor and a mortal wound to his heart. As the soldier fell, his comrades were initially unaware of his trauma because there were so many people in the press of the crowd. As the crowd recoiled from the bloody scene before them, the assailant made his getaway undetected. The death of this one Roman soldier resulted in more Roman reprisals than the death of eight Sadducees who had been targeted because of their congenial relationships with the Roman elites.

The "Sicarii" claimed a significant victory that day, to judge those who had opposed or resisted the movement towards Jewish independence. They believed God was pleased with their acts of self-declared heroism.

Pontius Pilate, the Roman Prefect, and Caiaphas, the Jewish High Priest at that time, hastily met and condemned these Zealots who had the audacity to attack both Romans and Jews. Pilate indicated there had to be an immediate response to answer these atrocities. Caiaphas could not argue with that, but he wanted to remind Pilate that eight of his Sanhedrin members had been assassinated, as well as the one Roman soldier.

Pilate didn't seem to care about the losses sustained by the Jewish aristocrats as much as he did the one Roman, a soldier he actually knew personally. He ordered his troops to be extra-vigilant and on guard. He then commissioned one of his Centurions to put together a strike force, one that could mete out retribution for these dastardly and cowardly attacks. Throughout the night, many Jews experienced beatings and severe mistreatment for being at the right place at the wrong time.

By the next morning, the Romans had arrested twenty Jewish men and interrogated them about what they knew. Not a single one could provide knowledge of the assaults, and none were guilty of any of the assassinations. Still, by that afternoon, all twenty of the men were hanging on Roman crosses.

Just to show who was in control.

Rather than diffusing the situation, Pilate made it a thousand times worse. Every Jew was outraged by the arbitrary and capricious retaliation against the innocent. Those members of the Sicarii who committed the murders were now questioned about whether their tactics were valid or misguided. But the cycle of violence just continued to churn until one day it would come to a head.

Oh, how the Jewish people longed for their Messiah to come and make this wickedness stop! Only He could make these injustices right because He would be God's divine messenger of Peace and Justice. "Oh, God," they prayed, "send us "The Deliverer!"

Simeon was at home in Cana when news came about the Jerusalem slaughters. He was ashamed of his people for escalating the violence, and he hated the Romans even more for callously and indiscriminately killing innocents. Those men who were crucified were not the *Sicarii* who perpetrated those crimes. They had just become "scapegoats" to assuage the Romans soldiers from doing even more dastardly things against the Jewish citizenry. There was no justice in Pilate's actions--just venom.

While still reeling from the Jerusalem bloodshed, Simeon and his family had a rare night at home with little to interfere. At the dinner table, Eleazar asked his parents a direct question.

"Abba, Mother, what do you think about this Teacher, Jesus of Nazareth? I heard today that one of my friends saw him heal a leper of his disease. Then Jesus told him not to tell anybody, like that's going to happen. Then my friend said Jesus told him to go show himself to the Priest and offer a sacrifice that Moses required when someone was a cleansed leper. That's amazing isn't it?"

The parents looked at each other wondering who would speak first. Simeon took the lead. "Well, son, that is an amazing story. Do you know why he was supposed to go and tell the Priest about it and offer a sacrifice?"

"No," said Eleazar.

"Moses wrote in the Pentateuch about how God wanted it handled if a person was a leper. First of all, they had to move out of their homes and live in a separate place, usually with other lepers. Leprosy is terribly contagious and

you don't want to get close to someone with leprosy. Have
you ever seen a leper?" Simeon asked.

Eleazar said, "Yes, once my friend Judah and I were
walking towards home and we heard a man yelling,
"Unclean! Unclean!" We immediately remembered our
Torah training and knew that meant the man was a leper
and warning us to stay away from him. Still, we wondered
if we had gotten too close. "Mother, do you remember I
told you about that incident when it happened?"

Martha nodded, affirmatively.

"It was very scary," Eleazar added.

"I'll bet," Simeon replied. "Since a person is a leper
and so contagious, the Law says he or she can no longer
participate in our religious activities. They are Unclean that
way, too. I've never heard of it happening, until now, but
Moses had a provision in the Law that if anyone was
cleansed of their disease, they had to go to the Priest for
inspection. After the Priest examined them for a week, if
they were indeed clean they could be reinstated into Jewish
society. They would offer an unusual sacrifice, taking a live
bird and then sacrificing another bird. They would dip the
live bird in the dead bird's blood and then let it fly away--
free."

The children looked on inquisitively.

Simeon continued, "Don't ask me, I don't understand
all those things. But that's what the Law required. So,
Eleazar, why do you think Jesus wanted the man to go to
the Priest first?"

"Well," Eleazar answered thoughtfully, "I guess he
wanted the man to get reinstated in the community. And
Jesus wanted him to do exactly what the Law required
relating to the sacrifices as a testimony to the Priests. He
wanted the man to be obedient to God's Law."

"Outstanding answer, Son," Simeon said, proudly. "That's exactly right. The man needed to do what the Law required. When he did, the Priest declared him cleansed, and he was able to go home to his family and friends. Wouldn't that be amazing?"

"Kind of like everything else Jesus does," added Martha, with a smile.

"By the way," said Eleazar, "My friend said Jesus reached out and touched the leper before he healed him. What do you think of that?"

Simeon seemed shocked at that information and paused before answering tentatively, "I'm not sure why he did that. Most people would never touch a leper. But Jesus did, is that right?"

"That's what my friend saw. And everybody jumped back when he did. Some people are saying Jesus is God. Is that possible?" he asked.

Simeon responded slowly, measuring his words, "I don't know. I haven't heard that before. He apparently does amazing miracles before many eyewitnesses, including your mother. But, God? I can't say for sure...Martha, anything you want to add at this point?"

Without hesitation, Martha said, "I think Jesus must be God, or at least he has God's power. Wouldn't that make him *like* God? One thing I know, only someone from God could do the miraculous things Jesus does. And reportedly, he has done much more. Did you hear about him walking on the water of the Sea of Galilee?"

"Ok, that's where we need to stop," interrupted Simeon. "I suppose we could go on for a long time recounting some of the things Jesus allegedly did. Did I tell you about the time I met Jesus?"

"What?" All the children responded in unison.

Martha hastily responded, "Oh, so *now* you are sure you met Jesus while working with him at Nazareth and Sepphoris?"

"Well, I'm pretty sure it was him," Simeon said. Everybody laughed as they prepared for their evening sleep.

Simeon slept restlessly that night. Questions swirled in his head, about Jesus, the Romans, the Zealots, and Barabbas and his family. There were so many important questions, but unfortunately, very few answers. Kind of like the question Eleazar asked about whether or not Jesus was God? Is it possible, He is the Messiah from God?

Oh, well, I must get some sleep, Simeon lamented.

CHAPTER SEVEN

A Zealot's Compassion

FOR WEEKS FOLLOWING the Jerusalem hostilities, people in Galilee were buzzing about what happened. Some of the people applauded the work of the *Sicarii* as they struck a blow against Roman imperialism, while also sending a message to those Jewish sympathizers who supported their oppressors. Others questioned whether or not those kinds of tactics would actually help alleviate burdens the Romans had placed on them. In the short-term, it added to the suffering and misery of the people, with innocent people being executed and families being destroyed. What value was really achieved by the Zealots if all it did was bring further persecution on God's chosen people?

Not only was Jerusalem politically tense after the Yom Kippur violence, but the religious leaders were also feeling threatened by a new phenomenon. A few years earlier, the Pharisees and Sadducees were challenged by a bold and fiery itinerant preacher in the Judean wilderness. People came to regard him as a Prophet from God. His name was John the Baptist. It had been more than 400 years since a true prophet had ministered in Judea, and the people saw in John those same dynamic qualities.

John had burst on the scene suddenly, demanding the people examine their own lives and practice piety towards God. He preached that everyone, after careful introspection, should repent and turn from their sinful ways and whole-heartedly reaffirm allegiance to Almighty God. He also encouraged those who had made that internal change to come to the Jordan River down around Jericho to in its waters. This ceremonial act of baptism was a symbol of a repentant life and a willingness to make God a priority in their family and worship.

At that time, the Pharisees and Sadducees (who rarely agreed on anything), sent representatives down to the Jordan to speak with John. He was confrontational when it came their hypocritical religion and compromising power grabs. But even though John powerfully exposed their flaws, they still wanted to have him answer one burning question--Was he the Messiah?

John vehemently denied that he was the Coming One, and even self-effacingly declared he was not even worthy to loosen the straps on the sandals of the true Savior. But a short time later, John, who considered himself the *forerunner* of the Anointed One, pointed to the one he identified as the *true* Messiah. On that day, Jesus of Nazareth came to John (his cousin) desiring baptism.

When John the Baptist saw Jesus approaching, he declared in the hearing of a large audience, "Behold, the Lamb of God who takes away the sin of the world!" Then, he reluctantly agreed to baptize Jesus, who wanted to validate John's public ministry and establish a precedent that, one day, this kind of baptism would be a practice for His followers, as well.

In those days, the religious leaders of the Jews saw in John a potential threat to their power base and control over the people, as well as their tenuous alliance with the Roman authorities. They were concerned that John threatened things that were quite fragile. But the question of John's influence was ultimately answered by a capricious act of the Tetrarch in Galilee, when John was arrested, imprisoned, and ultimately decapitated by the adulterous Herod Antipas.

With John silenced, the Jewish leaders hoped things would return to normal when it came to threats to their power. But just when they thought things were improving, a more direct and immediate threat emerged in the person of Jesus of Nazareth.

The first introduction of Jesus to the religious elite in Jerusalem occurred on his first visit to Jerusalem following the launch of his public ministry and his gathering of twelve key followers. Jesus took his followers to the Temple to observe the activities going on around the focal point of the Jewish religion.

What Jesus observed grieved him.

By this point, things in and around the Temple had become very materialistic. People would give ostentatious offerings with trumpets and fanfare so all the people could observe their generosity. They did it to be seen of men. It was one such show that triggered the debacle with the *Sicarii* and their vicious plan to kill people.

But other forces were also at work.

Years earlier, the protocol for Temple merchandising had been put in motion. Following Herod the Great's remodeling efforts, the expanded courtyard and Temple properties allowed for enhanced opportunities to market things related to Temple worship. All kinds of things were sold, purportedly to improve the worship experience.

Location was everything. To get a good spot to ply your wares would lead to making more money. Even the beggars at the Temple gates competed for the best place to pull on the heartstrings of worshippers. But, in fact, this merchandising bonanza was orchestrated and controlled by some leaders of the Sadducean Party.

During the administration of Gratus, the Prefect just prior to Pontius Pilate, a notable Sadducee by the name of Annas entered into in a financial relationship with the Governor. Annas paid a large bribe to gain approval for his son-in-law, Joseph Caiaphas, to serve as the High Priest. There were few spiritual qualifications for that office at that time. So, year after year, Annas would serve as the High Priest or secure the office for one of his relatives.

When Pontius Pilate took over, the bribes continued, now being directed to the new Prefect. Over the years, Annas, his sons Alexander and John, and his son-in-law Caiaphas, all enjoyed taking turns serving as High Priest. To control the High Priesthood, meant that you also controlled the activities associated with the Temple *concessions*. In other words, everyone who bought or sold things around the Temple had to pay a percentage to Annas to maintain their coveted location and lucrative business.

Some of the merchandising was directly related to Annas' financial control. For example, the "Jewish approved sacrifices" were for sale at the Temple Bazaar. If a family came to the Temple to offer an animal sacrifice, but they were unable to bring one with them, they could purchase one approved by the Priests. Often times these offerings would be double or triple the normal price, but everyone wanted to have a "spotless" animal to offer to God, right? So people would pay the cost in order to fulfill their sacrificial duties. Every time that happened, Annas and his family profited.

But there was another facet of this industry.

Jewish worshippers would come from all over the Roman Empire to participate in certain feast days. They often had Roman coinage. That was not "kosher" for the Temple, so they needed to convert their *denarii* into Jewish *shekels*. Needless to say, the person changing their money to Jewish currency always paid a premium transfer fee, in order to get the proper denominations. Each transaction created profit for Annas and company. No wonder he had no problem paying the bribe to the Prefect to maintain their cozy relationship.

So when Jesus entered the Temple confines through the Eastern Gate facing the Mount of Olives that first time since launching his public ministry, he was struck by the vulgar merchandising. The more he saw, the more passionate he became. He crafted a makeshift whip, not to injure anyone, but to exaggerate his motions, and he moved into action as his followers looked on with amazement. Jesus moved toward the money changers and toppled their tables, spraying coins all over the stone pavement. He then released the animals from their holding pens and threatened those who tried to intervene.

As he was making this powerful statement through his actions, he was also overheard repeatedly saying, *"My Father's House is a House of Prayer. But you have turned it into a den of thieves. Get out!"*

The zeal with which Jesus responded that day made some of the Zealots wonder if maybe Jesus was in agreement with them.

This was the first of two occasions when Jesus cleansed the Temple. Annas recognized the possible threat this young Rabbi posed to his fragile alliance with the Romans. One thing was clear, this rogue Rabbi was bad for business.

Jesus stayed only briefly in Jerusalem before retreating to his adopted home in Capernaum.

Back in Cana, Simeon and Martha learned some bad news. About six months earlier, Miriam, Simeon's mother, had passed away. The family was still grieving. But to add to the burden of her death, a messenger came to their home one afternoon to tell them about a heartbreaking incident. Martha's close friend, Lois the widow, had suffered a horrible tragedy in her home. Her only son Philip, the pride and joy of her life, had died suddenly. He was just 16-years-old. Martha fell to the ground weeping when she heard the news. She reeled and immediately began considering what she could do to help. Simeon and Martha had invested so much in helping Lois and Philip over the years she considered him like her own son.

Philip and Eleazar were close in age and had become good friends. Martha shuttered to think she was going to have to tell him about Philip's death. Simeon acted quickly, sending Martha and Eleazar to her parent's home, which was close to where Lois lived. As for Eleazar, he reacted predictably over the loss of his friend--with tears. Simeon knew Martha's father, Ephraim, would do all he could to help. If Martha was there she could certainly help with the preparation and burial of Lois' precious son.

Mother and son headed out on two donkeys the family-owned. It was less than a two-hour journey, so they would arrive before dark. They planned to go to Ephraim's home first. Simeon agreed to stay with the other children, not wanting them to have to deal with a funeral. Martha checked in with her parents and immediately made her way over to see Lois. Both Martha and Eleazar did their best to comfort their grief-stricken friend, but both of them were also struggling. How could this happen? They also questioned why Lois had faced so many heartaches in her life. How is it fair that she lose Philip? Oh, God, they wondered, *how can you receive glory from this terrible ordeal?*

Finally, everybody left Lois' home except for her friends from Cana. They all slept restlessly that night, if you could call it sleep at all. Lois and Martha talked way into the night before they felt like they could fall asleep. Though they were both exhausted, the grief of the day's events didn't let them sleep very much.

They all rose early so they could make final preparations to carry Philip's body to the family burial site, just outside of town. In the custom of the Jews, they would bury their dead within twenty-four hours. By mid-morning, family, friends, and mourners from the city were gathering outside Lois' humble home. She had already confessed to Martha how hard it was going to be to come back to that now hauntingly empty house.

She put Philip's best clothes on him, arranged his hair perfectly, and put his father's ring on his finger to take with him to the grave. Looking at his lifeless body once again caused her to break down and weep. People who were outside, hearing her wails, joined in with their own mournful laments. Martha and Eleazar also wept, again.

Ephraim and Martha's mother had arrived to escort the funeral procession to the burial site. Martha and Ephraim both provided frankincense for Lois, so she could add some perfume to the body and somewhat retard the process of decay. The sweet fragrance added to the waves of emotion that kept sweeping over Lois, as well as all those gathered. The meager preparations were made and everyone was there to accompany the widow and her fallen son to his final resting place.

They carefully placed Philip on a burial board, and several of the men, including Eleazar, carried him. Lois and Martha followed immediately behind, and then the other friends and loved ones. They all made their way to the burial site just outside the gate of the city of Nain.

Suddenly, a large group of men and women approached from the other direction. They were unaware of Philip's funeral procession. When they heard the noise of weeping they grew silent, realizing it was a death dirge. The crowd following the body was significant, indicating to the arriving visitors that this must have been someone important. In reality, it was because of the great number of people who loved Lois and lamented about her unbearable loss. As the group respectfully waited for the funeral procession to pass by, something unusual happened when one of the visitors said to Lois, "Don't cry."

It was audacious for a person standing there to make such a callous command. As Martha focused on the man who spoke, trying to fight back resentment for his comment, she thought he looked familiar. How did she know him? By this time the procession came to an uneasy pause. Even the people who had been lamenting stopped. As Martha looked toward the man, Lois leaned over to her and said through her tears, *"It's Jesus."*

She was right. It was the man at the wedding in Cana, the one who had turned water into wine. But why had Jesus commanded Lois to stop weeping? Surely, he understood the pain and grief of the her profound loss.

Jesus quietly moved over to the bier that held the body of Philip. All the men carrying it, including Eleazar, stood motionless. Martha and Lois looked into the eyes of Jesus and they immediately sensed his compassion. How kind, Martha thought, that Jesus would take the time to pay his condolences and express his genuine care for Lois and her loss. Jesus looked directly at Lois, who seemed buoyed by his loving glance, and then he refocused on Philip's body.

What Jesus did next stunned the crowd.

Jesus moved even closer to Philip and spoke, "Young man, I say unto you, ARISE!"

Suddenly, and inexplicably, Philip sat up, and spoke. "What is going on here? Who are you, sir?" He seemed to have simply awakened from a nap and couldn't figure out why this stranger was standing next to him or why all the people were nearby.

Martha felt Lois' knees buckle. Martha and Eleazar immediately stared at each other with amazement. As everyone stood in stunned silence--even Jesus' own friends--the profundity of the moment could not be grasped by any of the on-lookers. Jesus casually grabbed Philip's hand and helped him climb down from his funeral plank and stand up. Then, as if he did this sort of thing every day, Jesus walked him over to Lois and presented her son, to his mother. Lois stared at her resurrected son with bewilderment. Philip seemed confused by everything that was happening. The last thing he remembered was excruciating pain in his head and everything going black. Now, he was coming to realize, apparently this had been his funeral procession. Everyone in the crowd thought what they just witnessed, was unbelievable.

At first, fear seemed to overtake everyone in the multitude. Who could raise someone from the dead? They stood frozen in the moment trying to process what they had witnessed. There was an eerie silence. Then suddenly, Lois let out a shriek of pure joy as she embraced Philip and clung to his neck as if she would never let go.

Slowly, as if a wave washed over them, the crowd starting laughing and rejoicing and shouting, and they began to glorify God for this marvelous miracle. Jesus just stood there and smiled. What a wonderful reunion he had facilitated. His own disciples were leading the people in praise as they had just done the previous day when Jesus healed the centurion's servant who was near death in Capernaum.

Now, this widow's son in Nain was actually raised from the dead!

Of all the miraculous things his disciples had witnessed up to this point, this act of physical resurrection surpassed them all. Eleazar pushed his way through the crowd and embraced his mother. Leaning into her, he whispered, "Jesus really is God!" Martha continued to weep with joy for Lois and Philip. Martha nodded in agreement, pulling her own son in for a tighter hug. She was so glad he had been here to witness this profound moment. They would never forget this and it was a sure thing Lois and Philip would never forget it, either--even if he was still unsure what happened.

He also wondered what smelled so good.

Lois sufficiently gathered herself and realized she had to speak to Jesus. She briefly released Philip and together they made their way over to him. In a broken and barely audible voice, Lois said, "Thank You, Jesus."

Jesus gave her a comforting smile and acknowledged her effort to show her gratitude. Lois continued, "I know you are a Prophet sent from God, but after today, I know you are God. Hallelujah, for your amazing Grace and Mercy!"

Jesus, turned to walk away when Martha and Eleazar also caught up with him. Martha exuberantly said, "Jesus, thank you so much for helping my friend. She thought her life had just come to an end. Instead, her new life is just beginning. It's like she has been reborn! My son and I just wanted to tell you personally how thankful we are that you were here to perform this awesome miracle. We agree with Lois, we believe you are God in human form. Praise be to Jehovah!"

Jesus extended his arm and shook hands with an astonished Eleazar. Then Jesus and his entourage regrouped and continued their trek through the Valley of Jezreel. People from Nain watched until Jesus' and his entourage disappeared out of sight.

Filled with unforgettable memories of the day's events, everyone began to drift toward their homes. Each person took time to encourage Lois and express gratitude to have witnessed this marvelous act of God. Martha and Eleazar followed Lois and Philip to their home. As they talked, the young men behind them were being quite boisterous. No doubt, Eleazar was rehearsing all of the details of the last twenty-four hours with Philip. Certainly, some of the things they recounted about mourning over Philip's death, caused each of them to laugh heartily now that Philip was very much alive. Lois and Martha soaked in every moment.

Lois thought to herself, I never, ever expected to hear that laughter again.

Then came Jesus...

After animated goodbyes, Martha and Eleazar left Lois and Philip with assurances they would get together shortly. In fact, Martha insisted that the two come over to their home in Cana soon. Martha declared, "I want to be there when Simeon sees Philip for the first time. He always acts like he's so tough, but really he will be like a bowl of mush." They all laughed and agreed to a quick reunion. Martha and Eleazar shared their love with her parents and then left for home.

The two-hour donkey ride back to Cana passed quickly with animated reflections about the day's events. Neither of them could believe what they had seen and heard. Martha and Eleazar also talked much about Jesus. He had to be God to do the things only God could do. They wanted to know more about him.

It was just before the sunset when they approached their property. But even before they could get close to the house, Simeon, Lydia, and John came racing in their direction. "We heard, we heard, that Philip came back to life!" exclaimed Simeon. "The story is being told everywhere around here. You must tell us what happened. Were you both actually around when Jesus did this miracle? Did you witness it?"

"Woah, slow down," Martha said, while laughing. "Let's get unloaded and then we'll tell you all about it. Well, Eleazar can tell you all about it as he had a better view. Didn't you son?"

"Absolutely!" Eleazar beamed. "It was awesome, and I can't wait to tell you all about everything that happened. But maybe we should wait until tomorrow. I'm so tired now."

"No way!" cried his sister and brother.

"You can sleep in a day or two," said Simeon. "We want to hear every detail. Don't leave a single thing out." Before long they were all sitting around the fire as Eleazar and Martha shared details about the day that would be forever seared into their memories. Simeon, Lydia, and John hung on their every word.

Martha was very impressed with Eleazar's recall of the smallest details. He was turning into quite a storyteller. She could hardly interject a word because he was doing such a perfect job of recounting everything that happened. She was especially amazed at how her young son was sharing his faith in this Man from God--Jesus.

Eleazar repeatedly said that only God could do what Jesus did. Jesus must be God! That was his final witness to the events of the day. Simeon also applauded his son's ability to tell this story with such passion.

What he was saying about Jesus sure made sense, but Simeon still struggled with the concept of God becoming a man. Oh well, another theological question for another day. At long last, everybody agreed, it was definitely time to get some much needed sleep. Yet, as tired as they were, every member of the family struggled to sleep because of the profound implications of the ministry of this Nazarene Rabbi.

CHAPTER EIGHT

A Zealot is Exposed

FOR WEEKS, THE talk all around Galilee was about Jesus raising Philip from the dead. Simeon was quick to point out that his wife and son were eye witnesses to every detail. In fact, people had to tell him to stop repeating his boast, as if he were present. He reminded everyone of the Torah teaching that a husband and wife were one flesh, so in a way, he *was* there. But nobody bought that.

As fate would have it, Simeon saw Barabbas and the topic of Jesus came up. He desired Barabbas' take on Jesus. Did he think Jesus might be the Messiah? Barabbas admitted there were certainly a lot of people claiming to be witnesses to him feeding huge crowds and healing all kinds of people, including the blind and lame. Some said they saw Jesus walking on the water of Lake of Gennesaret, and others claimed they had seen him heal lepers. Obviously, the rumors were plentiful about him raising that boy from the dead.

"Hey, those aren't rumors. My wife and son were eye-witnesses to Philip being resurrected from the dead," Simeon said, defensively.

"Yeah, yeah," repeated Barabbas mockingly. "It sure would be handy having someone like that in a battle, because if people got killed, Jesus could just bring them back to life and they could keep on fighting. Now that would be a valuable asset!" the Zealot leader sneered.

But in fact, Barabbas still wasn't quite sure what to make of the whole deal. He thought maybe Jesus was too soft to be the Coming One. Jesus kept speaking about loving your neighbor and turning the other cheek. He said people should be peacemakers. Barabbas just wasn't sure that sounded like a strong enough leader.

Was Jesus the Messiah? Barabbas didn't know, but he wondered if Jesus might be a Zealot after hearing about his cleansing of the Temple with a scourge and how he frequently put the religious leaders in their place by pointing out that they were hypocrites. That sure resembled Zealot-like activity.

But in the final analysis, Barabbas concluded Jesus must not be the Messiah, or no doubt he would have sought them out and joined their resistance movement. Jesus could have easily found them if he wanted to, because a couple of their former members in Galilee, Simon the Zealot and Judas the Iscariot, were both members of his immediate entourage. They could have brought Jesus to Barabbas if he wanted to meet.

One particular comment discouraged Barabbas greatly from seeing Jesus as a kindred spirit. It had been reported to Barabbas that someone was present when Jesus said, "Give to Caesar the things that are Caesars', and to God the things that belong to God." No true Zealot would hold to that opinion about Caesar, taxes, and the support of Rome. No, Barabbas concluded, he didn't think Jesus was the real Messiah or he would have revealed himself before now.

While Barabbas was alone with Simeon, he gave him some important news. "You heard about the *Sicarii* attack on Yom Kippur, right?" Barabbas said, in almost a whisper, as if the walls had the ability to hear.

"Sure," Simeon's answered. "Everybody has."

"Well," Barabbas cautiously looked around to make sure no one else was nearby, "I was one of the ones who participated in that attack against the heathen Romans."

"No way" responded Simeon. "You couldn't have done that, you were around here, weren't you?"

"Don't you remember? I went with Micah down to see some of his family in Jericho. They are loyal to the cause after the massacre of Micah's family," Barabbas explained. "It was while I was there that they developed this plot to begin the insurrection. Since Jerusalem wasn't that far away, we picked Yom Kippur as the day to launch the attacks."

"What was your role?" Simeon asked Barabbas, with a tone of concern.

"I was initially just a backup--someone to help facilitate escapes," continued Barabbas. "But one of our leaders became gravely ill and I had to step into his primary role. We were supposed to try and target Roman soldiers, but they almost always stayed together. I happened to see one Roman target as he left his cohort just as the signal sounded. I managed to get next to him and thrust my *sica* into his heart between the harnesses of his armor. I could hardly breathe because of the adrenaline rushing through my body. Just like that, it was over, and I hastily made my escape out the Eastern Gate to our predetermined rendezvous point in Bethany. Everyone made it back without incident, and we all quietly went back to our normal responsibilities in order to disguise our involvement. You see--even *you* thought I was around here during that strike for freedom." Barabbas smiled.

"But what about those twenty innocent Jews Pilate slaughtered because of the subversive attack?" Simeon asked.

"That was indeed tragic, but there are always casualties in war ,and unfortunately those people suffered unfairly" Barabbas said, trying to justify himself. "Besides, it once again shows the evil and wickedness of Pilate and why the Romans must be stopped. Our freedom-fighters must prevail. Pontius Pilate and the Romans are the problem-- not us."

Simeon still wasn't convinced. "I know they're filled with hate and deserve judgment. But I can't help but think about all those innocent lives that were lost and the families that were destroyed that day. Maybe that judgment should come from God?"

Barabbas boldly countered, "We are the instrument of God's judgment!"

With that, the two men went their separate ways. But now Simeon struggled just knowing the details of the Yom Kippur massacre. He wished Barabbas had not told him.

He understood the growing hatred toward Pontius Pilate, who had originally come from Rome, drawn out of the Equestrian Order, which was the second level of

Roman diplomats. But Pilate had a friend in Rome--
Sejanus, prefect of the Praetorian Guard in Rome and one
of the most influential men in the city. He had helped
Pilate secure his post, hoping it would lead to more
important roles in the future.

Pontius Pilate replaced a Governor named Valerius Gratus
when he arrived in Judea in 26 AD. He would serve as
Prefect until 36 AD. A ten-year run in a place like Judea
was quite an accomplishment. Many of his predecessors
had only lasted a few years before being removed by the
Roman higher ups. To stay more than a decade in a hostile
and challenging place like Judea revealed Pilate as a shrewd
and politically savvy politician. He could be ruthless when
necessary, but also cunning in making alliances and
religious pacts with local Jewish pragmatists.

However, Pilate began his Judean term of service on
shaky ground.

One of the first official acts as Prefect was to march,
with his military forces in tow, from Caesarea Marittima to
Jerusalem. Unaware of the religious sensitivities of his new
subjects, he entered Jerusalem with placards of Emperor
Tiberius proudly on display. He was stunned by the
reaction as the Jerusalemites saw this as an egregious
breach of the Second Commandment--the one about not
making any graven images.

When the Jewish leaders explained why the people
had reacted so violently to his error, Pilate still was
reluctant to back down, believing it would show weakness.
Jewish leaders lodged a formal complaint to the Emperor
in Rome, who in turn ordered Pilate to remove the images
in order to maintain the peace.

Pilate made several more political mistakes that put him at odds with the Jewish leaders. At one point he built a major water delivery system from the highlands south of Jerusalem to the city. This Roman aqueduct supplied Jerusalem with an important water source. But when it was completed, it was discovered the primary user of this new water supply was the Temple. Water from the aqueduct was regularly used to clean the Temple platform and flush the blood from around the Jewish sacrificial altars, washing it down the back side of the Kidron Valley and into the Kidron Brook at the bottom of the valley.

This process significantly lowered the amount of water going to the city, as the Temple siphoned off the lion's share. When Pilate realized the Temple's monopolizing of the water, he insisted that the religious leaders contribute to paying for the building of the aqueduct. They vehemently denied they had any responsibility to pay for the water source. After unsuccessful negotiations to have the Jews pay their fair share, Pilate took some of his military forces to storm and rob the Temple treasury to confiscate the money he believed was owed to him.

Every Jewish adult male had to pay a half-shekel head tax every year to the treasury to help maintain the costs of operating all of the Temple activities. That is why the fund was there and why Pilate decided to plunder it. Well, the Jewish religious leaders saw in this action an egregious violation of Pilate's authority. Once again he was reported to Rome. The Emperor sent word back to Pilate for him to quit inciting the people to rebel, and he was warned if he couldn't maintain the peace he would be replaced. So, Pilate was feeling the heat of his job performance and wanted to impress Tiberius going forward.

But even Tiberius approved of Pilate's handling of the Yom Kippur hostilities. For the assassination of a Roman soldier, the Jewish people had to feel the sting of the Empire's power to crush any potential rebellion. The sacrificial crucifixions of twenty Jews seemed a fitting way to let the people know any insurrection against the Emperor would be met with swift and decisive action. No one had better launch a strike against Rome with the intent of raising up a new King in opposition to Caesar in Rome. If they did, the Tenth Legion of the Roman Army stood ready to swoop down from Syria and eliminate the Jewish race, if necessary.

Rebellion in occupied regions of the Empire was inconceivable.

The Zealot's assassination plot in Jerusalem had set things in motion that would one-day result in the existence of the entire nation being in question.

CHAPTER NINE

A Zealot's Wife

SIMEON HAD BECOME more and more unsettled about his involvement with the Zealots, ever since Barabbas had revealed his participation in the murders at Gideon Springs and the Yom Kippur atrocity. He wondered if he should--or even could--continue his affiliation. He still hated the Romans for what they did to his father and how they mistreated and killed so many innocent Jews. But perhaps the Zealot's approach was causing more hardship and fear among the Jewish people. Simeon was considering stepping back from active involvement with the group.

One beautiful fall day, he found himself with nothing pressing to do, so he proposed that he, Martha, Eleazar,

Lydia, and John, go to see Martha's parents in Nain. And she could also check up on Lois and Philip. Martha quickly agreed, so they harnessed the donkeys and took the family wagon to Ephraim's house.

The day started out perfectly, but it would turn into one that would forever reshape their destiny. After exchanging pleasantries with her parents throughout the morning, Martha and the children decided to take the short trip over to Lois' place. Ephraim asked Simeon to stay with him. He had some business issues to discuss.

When they arrived at Lois' home, they had a precious reunion. As always, their discussions quickly gravitated to Philip and the miracle and other stories about Jesus' miraculous works. Before long, however, there was a buzz of activity just outside the house. The children who had been playing outside came running in to tell Lois there was a woman who wanted to meet her. When the women exited the house, they saw a lovely Jewish woman standing with Micah, Simeon's friend from Magdala, the one who had suffered the tragic loss of his family.

Micah explained that he and several friends had come up from the Sea of Galilee area to sell some items and do some shopping in Nain. He introduced his friend Mary who wanted to meet and visit with Lois. It wasn't all that uncommon these days. She frequently had visitors stop by to hear her recount the story of Jesus raising Philip from the dead, even though that had happened months ago. Lois was eager to visit with Mary, as long as she understood there were other guests in her home. Mary seemed appreciative.

Micah excused himself and stated his intentions to go and visit with Ephraim and some other men. It struck Martha as odd that her father was now meeting with others besides Simeon. In fact, Martha felt a little uneasy that

Simeon may be getting trapped into something. But those anxieties quickly dissolved as Lois and Martha welcomed Mary.

The children followed to get a little snack.

Mary was quick to ask Lois to retell her miraculous encounter with Jesus. Little did Lois know, but the entire countryside was still abuzz about Jesus raising the widow's son from the dead. It was one of his most spectacular miracles yet. Martha was quick to interject that she and Eleazar were eye-witnesses to the whole thing. Mary seemed to hang on her every word. She nodded and sighed at each amazing detail. Lois never tired of sharing the story. And Martha had a way of adding color at just the right moment.

But soon the conversation turned to Mary.

"Mary, what's your interest in all these details?" Lois asked. "Are you also trying to figure out if Jesus is really the Messiah?"

Mary's immediate response surprised the two women and the children, all of whom were listening, "Oh, I *know* He's the Messiah. In fact, I know He's the Son of God!" The words seemed to startle the group.

After a few moments of stunned silence, Martha quietly asked, "What do you mean?"

Mary smiled and began to explain, "Well, I came here today to see Lois because of Jesus' now-famous miracle here. And you have also shared your testimony about Jesus' first miracle, because you were both present at the wedding in Cana. But I know Jesus, *personally*. And I've been an eye-witness to many of his miracles." "

Really?" Martha asked, as she glanced at Lois. The women wanted to know more.

"So you've been with Jesus and you've seen Him do these marvelous things many times?" Lois asked.

"Yes, Lois," declared Mary. "In fact, I'm one of His miracles, too."

"What does that mean?" Lois and Martha asked, in almost perfect unison.

"Well," Mary continued, "I was an invalid--out of my mind with voices and hauntings. People in Magdala were afraid of me. They said I was possessed by demons. And I think I was. I don't know how it happened, but I experienced constant oppression. I was slowly dying. Then one day, Jesus came to town. He heard about my hopeless condition, and for some reason, I still don't know why until this day, He came to my house. Immediately, my internal tormentors reacted to His voice."

Lois, Martha, the boys and Lydia, all sat there breathlessly.

Mary continued, "Jesus came over to me and touched my face in the gentlest way. He then commanded the demonic forces present in my life to immediately depart. I was thrown to the floor into convulsions as the powers of Satan were forced out of my body by the power of Jesus. Shortly after the ordeal, I clearly remember talking with Jesus and having my most lucid thoughts in years. He told me God had sent Him to deliver me from seven demons that had been driving me insane. I was in awe of what He had done, but even more amazed at His tender and loving manner with which He assured me that everything would be alright."

"Those are the exact feelings I had the day Jesus raised Philip from the dead," Lois said. "It was the most comforting peace I ever felt."

"Yes, yes," confirmed Mary, "That's the best way to explain it. Because of His loving and kind ways, and His powerful healing work, a confident peace settled over me. It's unexplainable except to someone who has experienced it." She continued, "The peace has continued until this day. Since then, I've become a disciple of Jesus. Because my parents, who passed away when I was young, left me a very large estate along with a significant fortune, I've been able to travel around with some of my friends, also women of means, to help take care of the needs of Jesus and His other disciples."

"What do you mean you are a disciple of Jesus?" asked Martha.

"Well, I'm one of His constant followers," Mary explained. "I listen to His teachings. I help Him any way I can. I testify about what great things Jesus has done for me. I get to witness many of the marvelous acts that Jesus does to validate that He is the Son of God--in fact, God, Himself--in human form."

"But you're a woman!" interrupted Martha.

Everyone laughed

After the snickering subsided, Mary affirmed, "Yes, I'm a woman. But that's the remarkable thing about Jesus' ministry. He's a Rabbi who treats all people equally. Everyone who follows Jesus is treated as His friend, with no distinctions. Now granted, He does travel at time with just the men of His group, because it is more appropriate that women not be in such conditions. But I've always felt as validated by Jesus as any male in the group. "

Everyone thought it was amazing.

"Mary, please tell us more about some of the miracles you have witnessed by Jesus, personally, besides your amazing story of deliverance," begged Philip. Both mothers were surprised to see the children so engaged in all of this.

"Well, I could go on and on, but I'll highlight a few of the most memorable," said Mary. "Not long ago, I was at home at Magdala, where I live near the Lake. Jesus, and

His twelve followers were in a boat crossing the Sea of Galilee. Suddenly, a violent storm overtook them. Sometimes, the violent winds come sweeping through the Valley of the Doves from the direction of the Great Sea. They can really churn up a tempest in the bowl shaped, mountain wrapped, Lake of Gennesaret. This particular storm was unlike anything I'd ever seen. It was a ferocious thunderstorm with torrential rains and vehement winds. I was fearful for Jesus and my friends on the Lake.

Even though many of them were experienced mariners, I doubt they had never seen a storm like it. I hoped they were safely ashore when the gale force winds raged. I later learned that they were right in the middle of it. As the storm raged, I venture out of my house to look out over the water, but I could barely see anything because of the driving rain. I whispered a prayer to God on behalf of my friends. Just as I was ready to make a hasty retreat back into the house, the most amazing thing happened.

Suddenly and dramatically everything became completely calm.

The rain stopped. The wind ceased. The most remarkable thing was that the waves that had been crashing on the shoreline as high as two or three cubits, suddenly laid down like glass. I had seen the opposite happen many times after a serious storm, when the winds ended but the waters remained churned up for half a day before they settled. But in this amazing moment, the waves ceased completely and there was nothing but an eerie calm.

I thought to myself, *What just happened?* I've never seen anything like this. I gazed out across the lake and it was like that everywhere. The thought immediately crossed my mind, *What did Jesus just do?*

The listeners were spellbound at Mary's account of the remarkable scene. Finally, Lois pushed out the words, "So what really happened?"

"I found out later," said Mary. "After my friends returned from the trip across the Sea of Galilee, I asked them about the monsoon they experienced that night. I wanted to know what was happening with them. I knew Jesus wouldn't say anything, so I sought out Andrew, one of the twelve. He told me the whole story. Jesus was so physically exhausted from his rigorous schedule, as soon as He got in the ship, He found a secure spot down low in the boat, and quickly fell sound asleep.

Several hours into the trip, Andrew said, the storm hit with remarkable force. They did their best to steer into the tempestuous waves, but it was almost impossible to do. They were taking on water, and no matter how hard they tried to row, their efforts were useless. Before long, they were in a circumstance that none of them had ever seen before.

They thought they were going to die.

To their amazement, Jesus was still asleep in the bottom of the boat. Finally, Peter woke Jesus up and asked Him directly, 'Master, don't you care that we are about to perish?' Jesus, woke up, quickly surveyed the situation, and then, to the astonishment of the twelve who were all hanging on for dear life, raised His arms toward heaven and spoke to the storm, 'Peace! Be still! Stop raging!'

At that instant, everything came to a dramatic calm, Andrew said. No wind. No rain. Even the waves stopped. It was over. Andrew alluded to the fact that Jesus had told them let's go to the other side of the Lake, so when they doubted His promise to get them there, He gave all of them a gentle rebuke, 'Oh, ye of little faith!' Andrew then told me about the awkward silence and the still trembling hearts of the disciples that had witnessed this miracle, and how they became 'Exceedingly fearful' after the storm was over.

I asked him what that meant. Andrew explained to me, when the storm was at its peak, they were very afraid. After Jesus calmed the storm with only His words, they were very afraid. Andrew then made this most remarkable statement, 'You want to know what's more fearful than the storm we were in? It's realizing that God was in your boat.' That idea frightened us more than anything. All of us were in the presence of God Himself, who could control even the winds and the waves.'"

"That's awesome," Eleazar shouted.

"Hallelujah," whispered Martha.

"That may be the most amazing thing I ever heard," said Lois. "No, wait that would be when Jesus raised Philip back to life." Everyone laughed at her quick pivot. But all agreed Mary's story was indeed phenomenal. Jesus was truly remarkable, if even nature would obey Him.

He must be God.

Mary said, "Do you want to hear one more? This one I witnessed, personally." Yes, they eagerly responded. "Well, Lois, Philip isn't the only person that Jesus has raised from the dead."

"Really?" Lois asked, with a tone of surprise.

Mary continued, "Not very many weeks ago, we were all in Capernaum with Jesus when He was approached by a well-known leader in the Capernaum Synagogue, a man named Jairus. The man fell down at His feet and begged him to come to his home because his twelve-year-old daughter, his only child, was gravely ill and close to death. Jesus immediately started to go with Jairus to answer the ruler's sincere request. But there was such a huge throng of people, they had to proceed very slowly. Suddenly, Jesus stopped and asked an unusual question, 'Who touched me?' Unbeknown to the rest of the crowd a woman had stealthily come up behind Jesus and touched the bottom of His garments. The woman had been very sick with a continuous issue of blood for more than twelve years. She had squandered all of her money with doctors and charlatans trying to get better, but her condition only grew worse.

So in a desperate effort, she did her best to get to the Galilean healer that everyone was talking about. Her intention was simply to touch Jesus believing that would result in her healing. So when she reached out to touch Him, the Lord felt 'virtue' leave His body, that's why He asked 'Who touched me?' Simon Peter quickly responded and pointed out the obvious issue that there were so many people how would it be possible to identify who it was that touched Him.

But Jesus knew it was someone who had done it with intentionality.

The woman meekly came forward and identified herself. Then she began to recount her story of being so ill all those years and only getting worse. In desperation, she had turned to what she considered her last and best hope--Jesus. The woman went on to say that as soon as she touched Him her issue of blood was immediately healed. Jesus smiled, encouraged her, and said, 'Your faith has made you whole; go in peace.'

Mary looked around the room to see if everyone was still listening. Everyone was hanging on every syllable. Mary continued, "All the while this impromptu delay had greatly concerned Jairus who was anxious about only one thing, getting Jesus to his daughter before she died. This unexpected interruption may have helped the woman with the issue of blood, but it had delayed Jesus from getting to

Jarius' house. When Jairus looked in the direction of his home an uneasy feeling gripped his heart.

Then he saw one of his family servants approaching quickly. Jairus braced himself for bad news. Indeed, the servant reported the girl had already died. Jairus was crushed by the news and tried to explain to Jesus it was already too late. But Jesus reassured him and said, 'Fear not: only believe, and everything will be Okay.' When they got to Jairus' home the grip of death was palpable. There were people mourning and wailing at the young girl's passing. When Jesus arrived, something happened that we had never seen before. Jesus tried to reassure those grieving when He told them, 'Don't weep; she is not dead, she's just asleep.'

The shocking thing was their reaction to Him. The entire group of mourners mocked Jesus mercilessly and scorned Him because of His comment. They knew she was dead. He hadn't even seen her and He was telling them she was only asleep. How foolish.

Jesus ignored their ridicule and invited Jairus and his wife, and three of His closest disciples, Simon Peter, James, and John, to come into the house with Him. Everyone else was asked to leave the room where the girl's body was. Even I had to remain outside with the other disciples," said Mary.

At this moment, Lois interrupted Mary's enthralling story and said, "I know exactly the feeling of that moment. Jesus told me to stop weeping and then moved towards my son's body as it lay there lifelessly. He was about to do something miraculous!"

Mary gave a tight-lipped smile and continued the story as it was related to her by one of the disciples who had gone inside with Jesus. "According to John, everything was settled and quiet except for the occasional sniffles of the girl's parents, still shocked by what appeared to be the death of their little girl. This was Jairus' first time seeing his daughter since he made his frantic trip to get Jesus. Now, it appeared to be too late. But Jesus had told him to 'only believe,' so he was doing his best.

Jesus looked in the direction of the pensive parents, then He walked over to the young girl's lifeless body and took her by the hand. He said, 'Child, arise!'

Immediately, life came back into her body and she sat up. Jesus escorted her to her parents and encouraged them to give her something to eat. Jairus and his wife were astonished and speechless and overjoyed all in the same instant. Jesus encouraged them not to tell anyone, but they could not contain themselves. It became known the moment they walked out of the house."

Then Mary resumed her eye-witness account, "I was waiting on the outside with the other disciples and those mocking skeptics. I remember the moment Jesus and Jairus, carrying his smiling daughter in his arms, entered the courtyard. Shock and awe was on every face. Those of us who were not surprised Jesus had done something miraculous simply began rejoicing and praising God for His amazing grace. If you could have seen the look on those arrogant scoffers, who were now confronted with the reality of Jesus and his ability to raise this girl back to life. They were dumbfounded. Soon the crowd started to join us in our jubilant praise and thanksgiving. Jesus had done it again--He had brought a dead person back to life!"

Once, again, Lois interjected, "I'm shaking with excitement, just to remember that exact moment when Jesus said to Philip, 'Young man, arise!' It was almost identical to what Jesus said to that young girl. Maybe, I understand better than anyone else, what this Jairus and his wife, felt at the moment Jesus did the miracle. I'm not sure anyone, who didn't experience it first hand from a parent's perspective, could possibly understand the profound emotions that accompanied that moment when Jesus raised our child back from the dead. He is truly God!"

Philip added, "Hearing you tell that story makes me understand a little better how my mother felt when she thought I was gone forever from her. For me, it seemed like just a second until I was sitting there with Jesus. But for my mother and others who were grieving it had to be a terrible ordeal thinking I was dead and never to return. But Jesus showed up. He can make the difference in every situation, can't He?"

Martha now spoke, "Amen, Mary. Thank you so much for sharing these most amazing stories about Jesus and what He's been doing. I have never been so captivated. You are a great story teller."

Mary smiled and said, "When they are stories about your own life and how Jesus has forever transformed you, all you are doing is being a witness of things you have seen and experienced. I am so excited to be able to share these testimonies. Jesus has made all the difference. Thank you all for being so hospitable to a complete stranger."

Lois replied, "You may have entered a stranger, but from now on we will consider you a close friend. I guess that's another thing that Jesus accomplishes. He brings people together so they feel like they're family."

Everyone smiled and nodded.

CHAPTER TEN

A Zealot is Trapped

THE WOMEN AND children were still in Nain and were reminiscing about their encounter with Mary Magdalene. It had been a most amazing meeting. But over at Ephraim's house a meeting of another sort had taken place.

Simeon had quickly accepted Ephraim's invitation to stay for some business discussions. He had always enjoyed fellowship with his father-in-law, and over the years their relationship had been very good. It all started with Martha's parents being sensitive to Simeon being fatherless, and they agreed to him marrying Martha without the ability to pay a dowry price. That had been such a blessing and set him and Martha on the path to a wonderful family life. Now that Simeon had become quite successful in his own right, he felt Ephraim was pleased with him as a son-in-law, someone who had provided very well for his daughter and the grandchildren.

Their conversations had occasionally turned political, regarding the Romans and the Zealots and all the problems in their nation. Most of the time they had been in agreement, but Ephraim seemed to be more opinionated in these later years of his life. He had embraced the Zealot cause even more passionately and felt the work of Barabbas and others was totally justified, even blessed by God. As Ephraim spoke that way, Simeon generally spoke softly and nodded in agreement. Honestly though, Simeon really didn't feel as passionately about the cause as he once had felt. Most of his feeling had been tempered by the violence and hatred displayed by both political sides. He just wasn't sure God was being honored by the killing of innocents by the Romans--or the Jews. Surely, God was able to raise someone up to deal with these major problems.

Simeon frequently wondered if that someone was Jesus.

Simeon and Ephraim were sharing pleasantries and refreshments when to Simeon's surprise, other men started showing up at the house. First to arrive was Micah, who related he had just left a friend, Mary, who was visiting with Lois and Martha. Simeon greeted his friend with a kiss on the cheek. Soon many other zealously-minded acquaintances arrived. Simeon felt a little uneasy in his heart about what seemed to be developing. This was by far the largest group of Zealots he had ever seen assembled. Then Ephraim's nephew Barabbas, the self-declared leader of the Zealots in Galilee, joined the group to cheers and applause.

Simeon was reserved.

After everyone arrived, Ephraim addressed his visitors. "Welcome, welcome, everyone. I want to thank you for coming to this rather hastily assembled meeting, but there are some pressing issues we need to discuss. We have refreshments and water here for anyone who wants anything. First, let me say that I'm proud of our freedom fighters who are making some important statements against the oppressive overlords. The Romans are a vermin in our country and a dishonor to our God. Every day we hear more and more about their atrocities and injustices against people. Just yesterday, we heard about a group of drunk Roman soldiers who robbed several homes north of Nazareth and Sepphoris. When some of our men resisted they were slaughtered by these heathen Gentiles. Of course, the Roman military people will ignore this atrocity and act like it was our fault for resisting. The injustice of it all!"

Everyone chimed in with hateful affirmations about the dogs who had perpetrated such atrocities. Their murmurs indicated something had to be done.

Ephraim continued his inspired challenge, "Those of us who love God and are zealous for the Law must act against such paganism and this blight upon our nation. Remember that in our past, less than two hundred years ago, when the ungodly Seleucids attacked with intentions of exterminating the Jewish people. Antiochus IV Epiphanes, their pagan king, captured God's Temple in Jerusalem and made it a shrine to himself. He offered a swine's flesh upon the altar of God and commanded the Jews to worship him as 'Theos Epiphanes,'--the 'manifest God.' Our Jewish forefathers changed his name to 'Epimanes' meaning 'Mad Man.' It was during those terribly dark days that zealous Jewish leaders stood up and fought against his tyranny. By God's miraculous provision and by the exploits of Judas Maccabeus we prevailed. After only three years of the Temple's defilement by Antiochus, our brothers defeated the great Seleucid army and recaptured the Temple, rededicating it to our God. We still celebrate that victory every time we observe Hanukkah. Our challenge today is every bit as great. These wicked Romans are set to destroy everything we hold dear about God, our Law, and our Land. If we do not zealously defend our nation and cast off the shackles of Roman rule our nation will be destroyed and our faith will be lost. You, my friends in this room, are the freedom-fighters our nation desperately deserves."

Ephraim's rousing speech caused most in the room to react with enthusiasm as they accepted their role as the primary defenders of the Jewish way of life. But for Simeon, this rally had turned into a referendum on whether or not he would continue supporting the Zealots and their causes. He felt the pride of his people and the need to protect God's chosen seed. However, he had doubts about whether the Zealot way was the *best* way to be a loyal Jew. These conflicted feelings gripped his heart as the assembly turned in a very sobering direction.

Simeon was about to be tested to his very core.

Barabbas had been waiting silently in the room as Ephraim spoke to the group. They had been sufficiently whipped into patriotic passion by the time Ephraim made his final comments and turned the meeting over to Barabbas for a discussion of strategy. Ephraim ended his remarks this way, "Finally my brethren, in my heartfelt opinion, the fate of the Jewish nation and the defense of Jehovah are at stake. If we will not be the first and best line of defense against these vicious attackers, then who will?"

The group now raucously indicated their agreement, although Simeon continued to be reserved. In fact, things started getting so loud that Martha's aging mother, the only woman in the house, was concerned the furor could be heard outside and might draw the attention of some Roman sympathizers in the area.

"Now friends," Ephraim concluded, "I want to turn this discussion over to the man I consider to be the head of the Zealot movement in our country. He has done more to inflict damage on our enemies than anyone else I know. We are fortunate to have him, but we must be careful to protect him and his identity. The Romans are on the lookout for our leader. They are afraid of him and his brilliant strategies. Let him know you support him and are willing to keep the resistance going. Welcome to my nephew--Barabbas!"

Shouts of approval followed and again the noise became dangerously boisterous.

Barabbas began, "Fellow liberators, it is my great honor to stand with you in our great national struggle. The religious leaders in Jerusalem worship at the altar of power, so they wink at the ungodliness and paganism of our task-masters. They have abandoned serving the true and living God and have compromised their own faith by befriending the Romans. They have an outward form of piety, but inwardly they are charlatans and hypocrites. How could they betray their fellow Jewish brothers by supporting the vicious oppressors? No, we can't count on them to make things better. Then there are those truly pious and faithful Jewish worshippers of God-- the Essenes. But their numbers are few and their strategy is to go out and live in the desert areas around the Dead Sea, practicing a sequestered and monastic kind of life that benefits no one. They are impressive in their devotion, but their answer to the Roman oppression is to ignore it. I predict that one day their passivism will result in their total destruction at the hands of the enemy they ignore. We cannot count on the Essenes to make any real difference in our struggle. So, my zealous army, I believe it is totally up to us to defend and liberate our nation from the heathen vermin who have polluted our countryside. The Roman presence is an increasing plague on our entire way of life. If they are the plague, then with Jehovah's help, we will be the *cure*." The thunderous applause and loud shouts of agreement added to the mob scene. At this point even Ephraim tried to calm the group down, fearing unwanted notice.

Barabbas, feeding off the passionate support of his audience, continued, "It is time to strike a crippling blow to our persecutors, one that will make them know they are facing an army from God who will bury them in the holy ground of our sacred lands." Again, there was an eruption of applause and shouts. But Ephraim had given up trying to restrain them.

Feeling he had satisfactorily captured the attention of the crowd, Barabbas began to lay out his strategy for their next bold move, "Brothers, I've been in talks with some rebels who are connected to our kinsmen in the resistance to Rome. They're from the Parthian Empire. I know in the past they have not been people we could count on, but you'll remember that in the past they helped destroy Antipater and Phasael, the idolatrous Idumeans."

Someone in the group spouted off, "Yeah, but that just gave us Herod the Great!" Undaunted, Barabbas continued, "I know, but this time it'll be different. The Parthians are willing to provide us with brand new weapons and support in our future struggles. It's impossible to initiate a true resistance if we don't have suitable weapons.

Of course, the problem is that we have to pay for such improvements, and we are not a wealthy group. But I have a plan. As you know, one of our own, Micah of Magdala, who perhaps more than anyone else has been afflicted by Roman atrocities, has family in Jericho. They've repeatedly housed members of our group and protected them when things have been especially precarious."

Simeon knew Barabbas was making reference to their escape after the Yom Kippur assault.

Barabbas continued, "Well, Micah and his family have spied out an easy way for us to secure the much needed funds and at the same time to deprive the Romans of gaining additional income from Jewish taxpayers. In Jericho, there is a Chief Tax-Collector named Zacchaeus. He is very wealthy and a noted traitor to our people. He not only collects the taxes in Jericho, but he has a whole network of agents who bring their receipts to him, and he deposits all the monies in his coffers. Micah's family knows that Zacchaeus will receive a huge deposit of funds on the first day, of the first month Nisan, just a couple of weeks before Passover. This will probably be the most money in Zacchaeus' possession at any one time in the year. There will be limited protection for him, and only a minor Roman presence in the area, so I believe it will be a great opportunity to attack the traitorous publicans and abscond with a huge profit, one that can fund our purchase of weapons. It will also deprive the Roman Emperor of his usual booty from the sacrifices of poor Jewish people."

More confident cheers.

Barabbas further explained, "Ephraim and I have been in deep discussions about this course of action. We believe it will be accomplished with the least amount of manpower and risk, and yet yield the best possible results. Therefore, I've decided to take four other men with me.

We will stable in Micah's home for a day or two prior to our strike. Obviously, Micah will be one of my selections." Hands shot up all around the room, those hoping to be selected for this most delicate and important mission. There were only a few abstentions, most notably Simeon.

Barabbas chose his men, calling them by name. "Aaron of Bethsaida. Andrew, the blacksmith. And Simeon, the carpenter from Cana." Simeon was stunned to hear his name. As he processed the whole thing, others were slapping him on the back and congratulating him for being one of the chosen. Everyone assured him that it was a great honor to be selected for this task.

As Simeon sat there in shocked silence, Barabbas concluded his appeal, "We need everyone to be ready to join the resistance as soon as we've secured the money and purchased our weapons from our Parthian allies. It goes without saying that these plans and strategies cannot be shared outside this room. Everything we're discussing must be kept completely secret to maintain the element of surprise and make sure the Romans don't intercept capture any of us along the way. One more time, let our Zealous Five know you are for them and will be praying to Jehovah on their behalf." Hallelujahs and Amens filled the room.

As the emboldened Zealots started to dispurse they continued to slap Simeon and the others on the back, thanking them for their service to the cause. Simeon never said a word to the well-wishers. He was, in fact, trying to figure out what to say to be released from such an obligation. There was no way he was the man for this task, especially since he had never engaged in any actual field work.

Simeon was anything but a soldier.

Soon everyone was gone except for Barabbas, the four chosen entourage members, and Ephraim. Simeon gathered himself and launched into his explanation why he should not be considered for such an important task.

"Ephraim, Barabbas, why in the world did you select me?" Simeon asked. "I'm probably the least qualified of anyone in the room! I have never participated in any of your operations, and I'm certainly not a fighter. I've even expressed some of my concerns about the efforts of the *Sicarii* and their extreme tactics. I just don't know why you think I'd be a good choice for the team."

Ephraim glanced at Barabbas and received an affirming nod from him on why he should be the one to explain. He began, "Simeon, you've been the perfect son-in-law and I love you like a son. You will remember when you first expressed your heart about Martha and your desire to marry her, I asked you some political questions, particularly about your stance toward the Romans. Your father had been killed by them and your feelings were quite strongly stated even though you did not know where I stood on the issue. You risked your whole opportunity to marry Martha with your passionate expression of hatred for the Romans. I was relieved to hear your position, and I think you were glad when I agreed with you. At that moment I knew we were kindred spirits and that you would make a great husband for my daughter. The reason we chose you for this mission is several-fold. First, you're a natural leader of men. You're a successful businessman and you have contacts as high up as Herod Antipas, although I know you don't approve of him and many of his positions. But you're an influencer, whether you know it or not. Second, we've been concerned about your commitment to the causes of the Zealots and we thought this would be a great way for you to demonstrate your support, and more importantly, your active participation as a vital member. We thought this would be an easy assignment with low risk and with other valiant men that would show your loyalty to the movement and enhance your standing with the others in the group. We both thought you were the perfect choice."

Simeon was taken back by their vote of confidence. Still, he was scrambling for a way to extricate himself from what he saw as a foolish venture. He countered with, "But Ephraim, what would happen to my family if something terrible goes wrong? Martha will never support me taking this dangerous step of escalating my involvement in the Zealot cause. I just don't see how I can do it. Please, can you find someone else to take my place, someone who's more passionate about this kind of action?"

Ephraim, still certain that Simeon was the perfect person for the job, let him think carefully about the great opportunity to become a Zealot hero. As Simeon still seemed to waffle, Ephraim played his trump card. "Son, do you remember the day you asked for Martha's hand in marriage? You may have to think back a bit, but do you recall the deal we made and the vow you vowed when I released you from the obligation of paying a dowry price for Martha? I told you, rather than pay a dowry, one day I may call on you to do a special project for me. When I redeem that promise, I hope you will respond with unhesitating affirmation and do what I ask of you. Do you remember your response to me in the excitement of that moment? You said, 'Absolutely!' Do you remember, son? Well, today I'm asking you to fulfill that vow to me and be a part of this special operation with Barabbas. Simeon, will you keep your word to me?"

It was as if Ephraim had punched him in the stomach. This question knocked the wind out of him. Yes, he did vaguely remember the commitment he made so many years ago, but he never thought it would come to something like this. His promise was exactly the way Ephraim recounted it, but he thought it would be to add a room on his house or something similarly benign, not open rebellion against the Roman government by participating in a raid like this. But what could he do? He had always been a man of his word, and he especially wanted to honor and please his Father-in-law. What would Martha say? Simeon looked in the direction of Ephraim and nodded his agreement in a half-hearted way. Ephraim quickly moved to his son-in-law's side and gave him an affirming hug. Simeon thought, *This day started out perfectly, but now it's a day that will forever reshape my families' destiny.*

Oh, how right he was!

CHAPTER ELEVEN

A Zealot Foiled

MARTHA'S REACTION WAS predictable and heated as Simeon explained what had happened during the impromptu meeting at her father's house. Her excitement from relating all of the things she had heard about Jesus from Mary Magdalene, suddenly seemed dulled by the news Simeon was sharing. Martha was furious, not at her entrapped husband, but at her father. How could he require Simeon to get involved in such a dangerous act of rebellion against the Romans? But, as they discussed every detail of the distant vow from the past, they both came to the same conclusion--Simeon had to fulfill it because he was an honorable man.

Oh, how he wished he had not made such a rash vow to Ephraim without being more specific about what might be expected of him. They decided they couldn't possibly tell the children about this without risking them accidentally telling someone else. At any rate, they could not fully comprehend the importance of Simeon fulfilling a vow he had made so many years earlier. The following days dragged on, and the uncertainty caused anxiety. Simeon's work suffered. He found it hard to focus on anything but the upcoming fearful task. He had a sense of foreboding about the whole thing, and he couldn't help but feel that it was going to be an ill-fated venture. Simeon did not know the details of his deployment, but he knew it was going to happen around the first day of Nisan.

And that day was rapidly approaching.

Finally, with only a few days left in the month of Adar, some news came from Barabbas. The five freedom fighters were going to meet at Ephraim's home the next day and make their trek down to Jericho. Prior to going over to Nain and Ephraim's rendezvous point, Simeon hugged Martha and tried to reassure her. She was crying and the children were unsure about what was going on. But when he gave each of them a near-smothering embrace and expressed his love, they knew something really important must be happening.

Eleazar received special instructions from his father. "Son, while I'm gone you are the man of the house. You take care of your mother and help with your brother and sister. Don't question her, just do what she says with a good attitude. I'm confident that you're a man who can watch over our family in my absence. I apologize for being distant and distracted the last few days. I was amazed to hear about the things you learned about Jesus from Mary Magdalene. I love you Eleazar, and I'm so proud of the man of faith you have become. Use that faith while I'm away, and take care our family."

Eleazar had the courage to blurt out, "But Abba, where are you going and why all the secrecy? Why is Mother crying? Are you alright?"

Simeon knew he had to give some kind of answer so he said, "Son, I have to do something to fulfill a vow I made many years ago. When you make a vow before God, it is imperative to be a man of your word and do your best to fulfil that vow. I must go today and take care of that promise. I will be gone for several days. I just hate to leave you all. I am fine physically, but what I must do requires a commitment I'm uncertain about being able to make. But I'm going to do my best to keep my promise, one that I made before God. And I'm sure He will have His will done, even if I'm unsure what that might look like. Do you understand why this is so important to me, Eleazar?"

Eleazar, still unsure of what was going on, nodded affirmatively. Simeon turned once more and gave Martha a long embrace before turning abruptly and walking in the direction of Nain. With Martha trying to stifle her weeping, and with the children teary-eyed, though not really knowing why, Simeon mustered up his waning strength and continued on his way with tears running down his cheeks, too.

Simeon was the last one to arrive at Ephraim's house. The other four seemed eager and ready to get on with this exciting mission. Simeon tried to appear engaged in the process, but he found it difficult to look in Ephraim's direction for very long. The older man was beginning to realize how much Simeon hated being a part of this undertaking and feeling he had to do it because he was trapped by his long-ago vow. Now, even the father-in-law was questioning if Simeon was the best man for the job.

The Zealous Five were not at Ephraim's house very long before they started out toward Jericho. As they departed, Ephraim leaned over and hugged Simeon, whispering, "I'm sorry I got you into this." Simeon thanked his father-in-law for trying to smooth things over. It was a three-day journey to Jericho. Each evening, the group made camp inconspicuously. Every discussion turned to the victory they were going to have, the money they were going to acquire, and the blow they were going to inflict upon the Romans. Everyone except Simeon seemed buoyed in spirit by each rehearsal of their plan. Simeon tried to appear as a team player, but it was hard to manufacture the adrenaline the others seemed to come by naturally. Simeon just kept trying to reassure himself it would all be over in a matter of days and then everything would go back to normal. But his nagging conscience kept whispering the question, "Will it really ever be the same?"

After pushing pretty hard on foot for three days, the men arrived in Jericho. It was a bustling city, and everyone seemed excited about the approaching of Passover up in Jerusalem in about two weeks. Many people were already preparing their sacrifices and offerings for their Temple visit. The five made their way over to Micah's family's estate, where several homes surrounded a large courtyard. This would be the group's home for the next couple of days before their operation. Most of Micah's family was aware of, and excited about, the proposed plan of attack. This made Simeon a little uneasy. He feared too many people were aware of their plans, even the timeline. But none of the others seemed to be concerned, so he told himself to stop worrying about it.

Barabbas seemed particularly charged with
enthusiasm about the raid. He reviewed the plan again and
again. To his mind it was fool-proof. The day before the
attack, the men were out looking over the lay out of their
target, when Zacchaeus, the arrogant Chief Tax Collector,
came by. Seeing him made everyone (except Simeon) feel
even more justified. The tax man was a vile traitor to his
people. He deserved everything he was about to get.

That night, they all slept restlessly because of the
adrenaline pumping through their veins, but Simeon found
it hard to sleep at all. Every time he closed his eyes, all he
could see was his beautiful family back in Cana. And he
couldn't escape the haunting feeling that he might never
see them again. He shuddered at the thought and had a
feeling of dread. His best way of coping was to rationalize
that it was just the fear of the unknown, and he would try
to force himself to get some rest.

But it was hopeless.

The next morning, they enjoyed a great breakfast of
various meats, eggs, breads, and salads, with water, milk
and juices to drink. It was a very special meal to energize
them for the task ahead. There was a little stir among the
family members present because a couple of the young
men had not returned home as expected. They were
coming back from Jerusalem the day before and hadn't
arrived at the anticipated time. Everyone just assumed they
didn't get away from Jerusalem as they had planned and
would be getting home later that day.

Nothing really distracted anyone from the mission at
hand--a glorious victory over the greedy tax collectors and
striking a blow to the occupiers, along the way. These funds
were going to purchase all the weapons necessary to launch
the ultimate insurrection against the Roman oppressors
and drive them from the land of Jehovah.

Today the rebellion begins.

Simeon and the others were in their places several hours before the actual attack. It was to be coordinated so when the publicans showed up to transfer their money to Zacchaeus, they would strike. They hoped there would be no bloodshed, but sometimes that can't be avoided when a battle starts. The long wait for the raid to begin was tedious, but now the trap was about to be sprung. The regional tax gatherers were making their way to the place of deposit. Oddly, Zacchaeus wasn't present, but his lead accountant was. Apparently, this was a standard tactic for Zacchaeus, who preferred to keep his hands off the money in public. There were only two lowly Roman soldiers standing off to the side to protect this exchange.

Simeon thought, *maybe this won't be so hard, after all.*

Barabbas spoke, "Simeon, you're with me. We'll go directly to the receipts table. Andrew and Aaron, you need to neutralize the soldiers to make sure they don't try to stop us. Micah, you bring up the wagon so we can load it and then make our escape. We'll meet up at the rendezvous point as soon as possible after the attack. Any questions?"

"This is going to be easy," Aaron said. "There's hardly anyone protecting the money. We are going to score big!"

Andrew chimed in, "No kidding. Come on men, let's do this!

Barabbas cautioned, "Don't get overconfident. Always be vigilant, because you never know when something can go wrong. Stay at your post and due your duty. Is everyone ready?" Everyone but Simeon gave a resounding, "Yes!" His "yes" was there--but just barely.

The true Zealots, plus Simeon, took their places. A large group of publicans arrived and laughed as they exchanged greetings. They enjoyed talking to each other because no one else would talk to them. So seeing each other once in a while was a social highlight. As the group placed their money boxes on the accountants table, Barabbas gave the signal to don their disguises.

Then they sprang into action.

Andrew and Aaron had the most challenging task--to neutralize the Roman soldiers. For trained military people these two guards were relatively easy to overcome. They hastily laid down their weapons, which Andrew and Aaron quickly collected. Then, with daggers pointed at their throats, the soldiers surrendered and got on their knees in front of their captors.

Andrew gave an approving nod to Barabbas indicating that things were under control. Micah then moved his horse-drawn wagon into position to receive the spoils as Barabbas and Simeon neutralized defensive efforts by the publicans. Most of them were already immobilized because their money boxes weighed them down. It's hard to reach for a sword or dagger when you're more concerned about your cash.

Several of the collectors had already deposited their boxes with the accountant, and their efforts to resist were very feeble. Just a couple of furtive moves by Barabbas completely halted any idea of fighting back. Barabbas ordered all of the depositors to place their money caches on the tables and back away.

Simeon immediately started shuffling boxes and moving them to a nearby wagon. He muttered to himself, "The sooner we get this stuff loaded, the quicker we can get out of here."

Barabbas was a little greedier. He wanted to see their spoils. He opened one of the money chests and gazed at the coins inside. But what he saw caused him to stare in disbelief. There was no gold or coinage at all. It was full of sand. Meanwhile, Simeon kept shuttling chests to the wagon. Barabbas quickly reached over to another money box and opened it. It was also full of sand. As if hit by a boulder, Barabbas was stunned. He tried to process what he had discovered.

While he was still in this dazed state, he heard something. So did Simeon. Roman soldiers were rushing out of every nearby building and tent, fully clad and ready for battle. Andrew and Aaron were the first casualties as the soldiers overwhelmed them with speed and accuracy. Shocked by what they saw, it was as if their feet were in quicksand as they tried to assume a ready fighting position. But the Roman swords were so swift and effective, Andrew and Aaron went down in a bloody heap. Simeon looked at Barabbas, who had just reached for his small sword, when four Romans pounced on him, wrestling him to the ground as he tried in vain to fight back. Both Simeon and Micah had barely moved when soldiers were right on top of them. Simeon had just glanced in Micah's direction when suddenly a club slammed against his head. Everything went black, and his last thought was, *I'm going to die!*

Unsure where he was--or when it was--Simeon realized he was still alive. His head was pounding and as he reached up to touch a tender spot on his scalp. He could fee oozing blood mixed with dry and matted blood in his hair. What had happened? His mind was muddled with fragments of thoughts. He couldn't readily discern between reality and foggy memories. He tried piecing the story together again, and he remembered the plan to rob the tax collectors. Suddenly, his mind was on a picture of Aaron and Andrew being repeatedly stabbed with swords and javelins. He just knew they were dead. This thing had gone so terribly wrong.

Barabbas and Micah? What about them? He wondered.

As he began surveying his surroundings, he realized he was in a darkened room, one with bars. He was in a jail and all alone. Did that mean his other friends had also been killed? For the first time, he tried to maneuver to a standing position from where he was on the cold, hard floor. His first efforts to stand were met by resistance from his legs, and his head pounded even more.

As he tried to steady himself against the stone hewn wall, he remembered thinking, *the stone mason didn't do too bad a job on these walls.* Wait! He was in a jail. Trying to focus across the expanse of the room, things were starting to become more clear. There was no furniture or any decorations. This was a plain cell, and it certainly wasn't built for creature comforts. As he started to peer beyond his cell door, it appeared there were other holding rooms. With that, it hit him: *Oh, no, I'm a prisoner!*

Straining to see outside, Simeon looked for evidence of other life. "Barabbas," he called out in a low voice, as even that effort caused his head to throb? Nothing. "Micah, are you there?". He heard a faint groan, but wasn't sure where it came from. "Micah?" he continued. This time there was no response. He was beginning to believe that maybe he was alone, and no one else had made it out alive. The thought also crossed his cloudy mind, *Does anyone even know I'm here?*

Suddenly, the room started to spin, and he slowly slumped to the floor, unconscious.

CHAPTER TWELVE

A Zealot is Guilty

BACK IN GALILEE, all those associated with the Zealots were restless to hear about what happened in Jericho. After several days with no news, Martha feared the worst and found it hard to sleep. By the time their loved ones should have made it back to Galilee, no one had heard a thing. That made Martha even more frantic. After a few more days, bits and pieces of what happened in Jericho were starting to tell the story for Martha and Ephraim and other Zealot Five family members.

Micah's family in Jericho knew some details, but they had been rousted by the Roman soldiers in the aftermath of the debacle. After all, two of their own had been killed as they resisted the Romans. A couple other members of

Micah's made their way to Nain to report to Ephraim. Martha was with her parents when the preliminary report was shared. The news was horrifying. Aaron and Andrew had been confirmed dead, killed by the military. Their fate was sealed very quickly. When Martha heard that, her heart sank. She was mortified and groaned. Breathless, she tried to focus on the rest of their news. The cousins had no idea what had happened to the other three Zealots.

Rumors were flying around in the aftermath of the strike but facts were scarce. They calculated that most likely scenario was that the three had been captured alive and hauled away to Jerusalem. There were definitely no bodies recovered, other than Andrew and Aaron. The details were so sparse that all those hearing about it reeled with confusion and felt hopeless.

With Martha's premonitions confirmed, she found herself slipping into a state of numb discouragement. She remembered firing a hostile stare in the direction of her father. His eyes looked down to the ground as he realized how much his actions had hurt his daughter and the rest of the family. What could they possibly do now but wait for more details? Martha wondered if she was ever going to wake up from this terrible nightmare.

Simeon, Barabbas, and Micah did indeed end up in the same cell block, where they had some limited contact, that is, when they were not being directly guarded by Roman soldiers. Each of them had suffered serious injuries during their arrest and transport. Simeon's head was lacerated and a blow to his skull had resulted in a significant concussion, rendering him comatose for a day and a half. Barabbas had attempted to resist his captors when first attacked, but was immediately overwhelmed by soldiers who soundly beat him before he, too, was rendered unconscious. Micah had been dragged off the wagon, carrying the boxes of sand, and similarly bruised and battered by his arresters. Every breath was painful, he was fairly sure he had a few broken ribs. But he was the only one who maintained at least some degree of consciousness during the ordeal, and therefore he knew some of the details about where they had been transported.

As it turned out, they had been taken seventeen miles from Jericho up to Jerusalem and incarcerated in the Roman fortress of Antonia. As they were awaiting their fate, Micah tried to piece together the reasons why their mission had failed so miserably. Once they all emerged from their various degrees of incapacitation, they discovered they were in close enough proximity to communicate. As soon as the Roman guards left them alone for a time, Micah tried to tell his two compatriots what he knew about their plight.

Micah whispered as loudly as possible, "Barabbas, Simeon, are you guys alright?"

Barabbas responded first, "I'm hurting but I'll live. You?"

Micah replied, "Yeah, my ribs are sore from the beatings, but I'll make it, too."

Now Simeon jumped in, "I have a head wound and was out of it for a time. Otherwise, I'm Okay. Micah how long has it been since we were brought here?"

"We've been here almost three days now. They carried us up to Antonia in Jerusalem. That's where we are, but I have no idea what's going to happen next. Did they leave you some water and bread in your cells?"

Both men said about the same thing, "Yes, I'm just now feeling I can eat something."

Micah continued, "I've spoken with some of the Roman soldiers who have been guarding us from time to time and brought in the food and water. They rather boastfully shared part of what happened in Jericho."

"Tell us!" Barabbas blurted out.

"Well, apparently, my two cousins, who didn't make it home the evening before our mission, were apprehended by the Romans while coming back down to Jericho. The Romans had suspicions about an attack and plied them for information. When tortured, one of them gave up details about our plan. So the Romans were lying in wait, ready to foil our plot."

"Do you know what happened to your cousins?" asked Simeon.

"No idea, but it can't be good," Micah answered. He continued, "They told the tax collectors to keep their planned agenda, but to substitute sand in their cash boxes for the money. Then the Romans deployed their strike troops early into their hiding places and waited for us. When we launched our attack, they waited to make sure all of us were fully engaged before they responded.

Since a couple of their Roman soldiers were being held at knife point by Andrew and Aaron, that became the focal point of their counterattack, and our friends were immediately killed in the ensuing violence. Then, we were brutalized and hauled up here to Jerusalem."

"Any word about what happens next?" questioned Barabbas?

"Nothing that I know for sure," said Micah. "But I did overhear the guards laughing about a public crucifixion that is supposed to take place sometime soon."

Silence prevailed after that comment. Simeon contemplated that outcome. It was so reminiscent of his own father's death at the hands of the Romans, and how several of his allies were crucified in the aftermath of that failed robbery so many years earlier. His mind raced to

Martha and the children. Oh, how sorry he was that they were having to cope with this terrible ordeal. He also thought about Ephraim and how he held Simeon to that vow he had made as a young man in love with Martha.

Now, look how all of those plans were working out. Simeon tried to resist the temptation to be bitter towards his father-in-law, but he was struggling. Then, quickly, his mind pivoted back to Martha and his kids. He started quietly weeping about their plight--and his.

On another front, the Romans were ecstatic over their efforts to foil the terrorist plot. They were quite pleased with their intelligence and the results. Pontius Pilate had been briefed on the whole military strategy beforehand and had sanctioned the plan to thwart the attack in Jericho. He took special delight that no Romans were injured during the action, that some of the rebels had been killed, and that some of the Zealots had been captured. He was contemplating the best way to handle their demise, a way to send the loudest possible message to other would-be terrorists. Crucifixion during a highly visible holiday might be just the trick.

And Passover was just around the corner.

That first night back in Galilee after hearing the dreadful news, Martha huddled with her kids and tried to control her weeping as she agonized through another sleep-deprived night. "Oh, God," she prayed, "please have your will done in Simeon's life. And please don't let him lose hope!" Emotionally exhausted, she finally slipped into a light sleep.

But it would be fleeting.

Chapter Thirteen

A Zealot is Afraid

THE NEXT MORNING, Martha started pondering how she could find out more about Simeon's status in Jerusalem, as well as his plight. It was a three or four day journey on horseback to get to the capital. She needed to determine if that was her best course of action, but communication was so slow, things could come to a head there before she knew anything. Her friend Lois knew of another possible way for Martha to get faster and better communication from Jerusalem.

Lois and Martha made their way to a man who lived near Cana and Nain.

His name was Joshua of Gilboa, and he had an interesting hobby that had turned into a lucrative business.

Joshua raised and trained Homing Pigeons. These special birds had the uncanny ability to immediately ascertain their geographical position, no matter where they were, and hone in on their home base even if it was hundreds of miles away. Also known as Carrier Pigeons, they could transport small messages in specially prepared tubes fastened safely to their legs. Then, when the pigeon was released somewhere else in the country they could fly the note to its home roost. This way, news could be spread within hours rather than days.

Joshua had many of his birds transported to Jerusalem, leaving them in the care of his friend and partner, Isaac. In like manner, he had brought several of Isaac's pigeons up to Galilee so, when needed, they could be released to fly south. This way several messages could be exchanged and answered in a single day. It was a costly system, but financial things didn't matter to Martha.

When the two women met with Joshua, he told them that he would be eager to help. He had done business with Simeon in the past, and he wanted to help Martha get information that might help her find out about Simeon's whereabouts. After explaining how his business worked, Joshua asked Martha if she wanted to do this. Martha's answer was swift and passionate, "Yes, let's do it! Here's the money, and if you need more, just let me know. What do I need to do now?" She handed him ten denarii--a substantial sum--but worth it to her.

Joshua explained, "I'll send a message to Isaac and ask him to investigate what's happening to your husband. But I'm sure his access will be somewhat limited. He'll probably have to bribe some soldiers. That may be expensive."

"I don't care! Please can we just do this?" Martha blurted out.

A little taken back by Martha's pointed response, Joshua wrote out a note asking Isaac to go near the fortress of Antonia and do his best to get some information about Simeon the Mason from Cana. "He had been taken in Jericho with a group of Zealots. Where was Simeon located and what was his health condition? Was there any news about his future disposition? Please respond as soon as possible because the matter was urgent!"

After finishing the note, Joshua carefully rolled the mini-scroll and placed it in the container on the pigeon's leg. Confident he had secured the message, he tenderly engulfed the bird in his hands, lifted it to the heavens, and tossed it into the air. The pigeon circled twice overhead, then, after getting its bearings, it made a bee-line due south in the direction of Jerusalem. In a few moments the bird was out of sight.

Now came the hard part--waiting for a response.

Martha asked two pertinent questions, "Is there some reason the pigeon may not make it to its destination? And how soon will we get an answer?"

Joshua responded cautiously, so as not to over alarm the frantic wife, "Well, they almost always get through to Isaac, and it will take a couple of hours to reach its home destination."

Martha reacted, "What do you mean they *almost* always get through?"

"Honestly, it's almost a sure thing, but we have lost birds to hawks. Pigeons are a favorite meal for the birds of prey, and occasionally, they get pirated away as they make their journey. The bad part is, we don't know for some time that we've lost a bird between here and their destination," Joshua said.

"Oh, I see," said Martha, pensively. "How long before we should expect a response?"

"It all depends on how quickly Isaac finds his homing pigeon," said Joshua. "He's not likely standing there watching when the bird gets there. But the pigeon will land at a special entry point to the coop, and Isaac will see a new bird has arrived as soon as he checks the pigeons to feed them. He'll see the message and act quickly, I'm sure. Then he'll have to go and do his investigation and bribe whomever he needs to in order to get some answers. When he has the details we need, he'll write his note to us, place it with one of my pigeons, and send it back to me. We should have some answers in about two hours after that. But based upon the time we've initiated this action and what Isaac has to do in Jerusalem, I can't imagine my pigeon getting back here before tomorrow morning. So, we should all probably eat and get some rest and look for our answers first thing tomorrow. Do you ladies have a place to stay tonight?"

The women had not really considered the possibility of having to wait until the next day. The children were safely at Lois' house, and they were old enough to stay by themselves, so they were aware their mothers might not make it back that night. Besides, Ephraim didn't live very far away in case of an emergency. Martha answered Joshua, "No, we really haven't made plans."

Joshua said, "It's settled then. You ladies can come to my parent's home with my family. They have multiple rooms where you can stay. It's just down the road a short distance, and I know they'd love to have you."

Martha and Lois followed Joshua to his home. They met his parents, his wife, and their four-year-old son. After sharing an evening meal and enjoying the hospitality, Martha excused herself and made her way to get some rest. Throughout the evening festivities, Martha's mind had been far away. What was Simeon doing? Was he all right?

Would the Roman's treat him fairly? At that thought, she shuddered knowing there was little likelihood of that. Since Andrew and Aaron had been killed, Martha realized that botched mission was a major incident to the Romans.

Suddenly, a fleeting hope flashed through Martha's mind. She remembered a custom that Pontius Pilate had initiated during his governorship. At the time of Passover, Pilate would make a gesture of conciliation and appeasement to the Jewish people by releasing a prisoner back into society and declaring that person pardoned Is it possible that maybe Simeon would receive that benevolent treatment? Since he had never been involved in anything like this before, maybe Simeon would be freed to return to his family. But just as quickly as Martha developed that thought, it changed into an intense foreboding, believing something ominous lay ahead. Maybe tomorrow would bring some answers. One more night of exhausting anxiety and transitory sleep.

"Oh, God," she prayed, "Please give Simeon peace tonight!"

Meanwhile, the prisoner Simeon's thoughts that same evening were anxious and pessimistic. There was still no indication from the Romans about what was going to happen next. They had given the three Galilean prisoners food and water, but not much else. The guards had not mistreated them all that much, except for Barabbas. Apparently, there was a rumor among the Romans that Barabbas may have been responsible for killing some soldiers in the past. In fact, one of the stories suggested he had been involved in the Yom Kippur terrorist activities. Even the possibility that was true made the guards treat him with disdain. A powerful blow to his head or body was a regular occurrence. Barabbas was on the receiving end of some additional harassment for sure.

The soldiers gave the men very little information, except to let them know the Jews had just completed their Sabbath, which meant they were entering into Passover Week. Simeon had also pondered the "custom" that Pontius Pilate had practiced during his tenure as Prefect. Maybe, he would receive mercy and be pardoned by the governor. It seemed so far-fetched to even consider that possibility. But a man has to dream, right?

All of a sudden, Simeon had an unusual peace come over him. No matter what happened, he believed everything was going to be alright. With that surge of optimism, Simeon managed a few hours of sleep.

Martha's morning started early as the sun was barely rising over the Galilean hills. She was able to eat a little of the breakfast provided by Joshua's family, but her real desire was to check on the pigeons. She and Lois followed closely behind Joshua as they made their way to the roost. Joshua tried to tamp down their expectations, but as they approached the pigeon coop, he excitedly said, "Hey, one of my pigeons is back! I'm sure it's from Isaac."

They hastily retrieved the bird and unfurled its scroll-like message. Joshua didn't read it out loud immediately until he had deciphered its contents. Martha waited breathlessly for the report. Finally, Joshua started reading, *"Joshua, I was able to find out a few things about your friend Simeon. He is alive and in a prison cell at Antonia. There are three men there. No one is seriously hurt. The guards believe the three are condemned to be crucified this Friday, before the next Sabbath Day. Sorry."*

The words of condemnation crashed into Martha like a raging bull. She fell to the ground, as if she had been shot in the heart. And in a sense, she had been. She could not control her sobbing, no matter how hard she tried. Lois closed in tightly, embracing her friend and trying to console her. But it was no use. Lois remembered a time, not so long ago, when Martha had hugged her in an effort to comfort her when Philip died. That's when Jesus showed up. Maybe Jesus will show up again in order to help Simeon. But that seemed unlikely.

As Martha began to compose herself, she looked at Lois and said, "We need to go." She thanked Joshua for all his help and hospitality and gave him ten denarii for any expenses they may have incurred. Then they started heading back to Nain.

Every step just seemed to intensify the fact they were getting closer and closer to Friday. With each accelerating pace, Martha was whispering a prayer to Jehovah, asking for His intervention and salvation. Lois could barely keep up with Martha's determined pace.

Martha was formulating a plan.

CHAPTER FOURTEEN

A Zealot Waits

WHEN MARTHA AND Lois got back to Nain it was the middle of a cool and beautiful spring day. It was hard to believe everything was so beautiful in nature, when people's worlds were collapsing all around them. When they got to Lois' house, they embraced and Lois promised, "I will be praying for you." Martha retrieved her children and immediately went to her father's home.

They still found it hard to look at one another since the Jericho debacle, but Martha needed her father's help. After recounting the events of the last two days, and sharing about Simeon's looming demise, Martha said she needed to go to Jerusalem to see if she might be able to get a glimpse of Simeon and reassure him of her love and devotion. Ephraim agreed to help her in any way possible. Ephraim had a nice wagon for traveling, and he insisted Martha take it with two of his horses for the journey to Jerusalem. She debated about taking the children but feared the horror of a crucifixion might be too much for the little ones. No, she would take Eleazar, and leave Lydia and John with her parents.

Not wanting to waste any more time, Martha hastily packed a bag for herself and her eldest son, while Ephraim and his servants got the horses and wagon ready. Martha's mother put together some bread, fruit, and water for the journey. That was all they would need. They could buy other commodities, if necessary. Martha gave her children a long and passionate embrace. They all cried, but she reassured them, "Jehovah is in control."

When she hugged her parents, Ephraim said to Martha, "I'm so sorry I've created this mess! I will never forgive myself for making Simeon do this deed, just to fulfill the fantasies of an old man. Now, I've lost my daughter too. I'm so sorry, Martha" he said, as he began to weep.

"You have not lost me," Martha forced out the words. "Father, I forgive you for asking Simeon to do this thing. He felt like he had to honor his word to you, but he still could have said no to this foolish thing. Now, it's in God's hands and we'll just keep praying for Simeon's deliverance, somehow. I love you, Father, and I don't want you to feel guilty over this matter." Ephraim suppressed a guttural groan at the relief he felt over Martha's words.

With that, Martha and Eleazar boarded the wagon and began the seventy-mile trek to Jerusalem. Lois had told Martha of some family friends in Jerusalem who would offer them hospitality when they arrived. She carefully explained how Martha could locate their home on the

Mount of Olives. Martha knew the area a little because of Simeon's annual trips to the Temple to offer sacrifices during Passover. Because they got away rather late that first day, they were able to make it to Beth Shean, south of the Sea of Galilee that first night. They two slept under the stars in the back of the wagon. Sleeping was difficult to come by for both of them. Martha was glad Eleazer had accompanied her.

As they traveled the next day, there was plenty of time to talk. Certainly, Simeon was the main focus of their discussions as they each shared memories about his winsome way.

They laughed--and cried.

After a while, the conversation turned to talking about Jesus' latest exploits. Eleazar was the one who first started discussing His fame, "Did you hear what Jesus did before He went down to Jerusalem?"

"No what?"

"Well, He continued healing people, making the blind see, the lame walk, and the deaf hear. Amazing, huh?" Martha nodded and smiled.

Then she asked, "Why do you think Jesus does all of these miracles? I know it's a blessing to those He touches, but why does He do them? What's He trying to prove?"

Eleazar responded thoughtfully. "I think Jesus does all of these miraculous things to prove He's from God. Otherwise, why would people listen to some new guy with a religious background? But when Jesus starts doing amazing miracles, signs, and wonders, I think that makes Him *divine*. His words now must be listened to because He has validated that He's from God. But I think it recently has to do more about His teachings."

"What do you mean?" Martha asked.

"Jesus is teaching things that are so different from the Scribes, Pharisees, and Rabbis. He teaches with authority, and everyone that I've talked to who has actually heard Jesus, says He puts all of the religious leaders to shame for not practicing *true* religion. He calls those Jewish leaders who say the people should live one way, but they live another way, 'Hypocrites.' That's pretty strong, isn't it?"

Martha continued to nod in affirmation. All the while she was thinking how proud she was of Eleazar for being so mature and discerning. If only Simeon could see him now. He would also be so proud of the young man Eleazar was becoming. And much of his growth had to do with his encounters, or the examples he had heard about, related to Jesus. She was so pleased with her son's spiritual insight, too.

Eleazar went on and on talking about the teachings of Jesus. Martha listened, admiring the wisdom and recall of her son, as well as his passion for Jesus. She was so glad he was more interested in Jesus than he was in the Zealot movement. If only Simeon had met Jesus personally, as an adult, maybe the trajectory of his life would have changed too. Then a thought flashed through her mind--*I wonder if Jesus might be able to help Simeon?* The answer flashed just as quickly, *No, I'm sure He has too many other important things to do than to worry about a criminal facing a Roman cross.*

About that time, Eleazar started winding down, especially when he saw the distant look in his mother's eyes. He knew exactly what she was preoccupied with--his Abba. It seemed like a good time for them to stop and eat something, water and feed the horses, and try to get some sleep. The next day they should get to Jerusalem. That was going to be a huge emotional moment as they would hopefully learn more about Simeon's plight. Eleazar bid his mother good night and told her to try to get some much needed rest. Eleazar was worried about Martha's health. She was so exhausted, she really needed some restful sleep. Maybe, it was because they were getting closer to where Simeon was, or perhaps because of the encouraging words shared by Eleazar about Jesus, Martha rested better that night than she had in weeks.

Rising a little after sunrise, Martha and Eleazar harnessed the horses to the wagon after feeding and watering them. They left early, fully anticipating they would make Jerusalem before sunset. They were making good time, but they noticed the foot traffic as well as others on horseback or donkeys, or even camels, were joining them along the way. Everyone was heading to the capital and the Temple to offer sin offerings for Passover. The road was getting quite crowded.

As they passed by Jericho, a cold sensation swept over both of them as they realized this is where everything had gone horribly wrong for Simeon and the others. It all just seemed so evil. From Jericho, the road up to Jerusalem made a steep grade from below sea level, up to David's City, which was about twenty-five hundred feet above Sea Level. All this took place within a 17-mile stretch of road. But the ancient road wound its way through a deep valley leading up to Jerusalem. Most of the time people traveling this highway were in the depths of the gorge that placed them in shadows with hardly any sunlight reaching the bottom. As Martha and her son negotiated their way through this dry riverbed in the eerie darkness. Again, she felt the oppression of an evil wind.

Then Martha recalled the words of Israel's greatest King, David, who wrote in Psalm 23, *"Though I walk through the valley of the shadow of death, I will fear no evil."* Martha remembered her early lessons from her father along this road. They were traveling this path that the Jewish people called, "the Valley of the Shadow of Death." Martha prayed within herself, *Oh, Jehovah, please keep me from the fear of things to come in Simeon's life. Let me remember, Your rod and Your staff will always comfort me. Please comfort him right now too.*

Simeon and his two fellow-prisoners were beginning to come to grips with their impending fate. It was now Wednesday of Passover Week, and through the small slits at the top of their cell, where a little fresh air could be gleaned, noises of the pilgrims over near the Temple were getting more obvious. The festive sounds of the travelers who had come to offer sacrifices to God and participate in the Passover Meal, were becoming more pronounced as they got closer to Friday, when the High Priest would offer a lamb for the entire nation. The Galilean Zealots were not sure when, but the guards had been slipping them hints about their inevitable fate.

Simeon, unaware that Martha and Eleazar were on their way, was losing hope by the moment. He just knew he was going to die, alone, helpless, and soon forgotten. He had made a choice that he could never reverse, and now eternity was imminent.

Meanwhile, in the other part of Antonia, Pontius Pilate was considering when he should publicly execute those captured in the Jericho fiasco. He and his military men were proud of their strategy to stop the Zealots, men

Pilate considered to be parasites on his Province. Indeed, he planned to make a spectacle of them, and he wanted to do it when the deterrent effect would be most pronounced.

He had already ordered his carpenters to prepare three new crosses. Since these crucifixions were going to be during the Jewish celebration of their Passover, he wanted the death instruments to be clean and pristine. Pilate thought doing it during their holy days would provide the most humiliating message for the Jews and their Zealot party. He had decided on Friday, that's when the most pilgrims would be in town and when the religious groups would be most chaotic. He was going to give them a not-so-subtle insult by killing some of their freedom-fighters on one of the days they most highly valued. Pilate also decided that custom where he tried to pacify the Jews by releasing a prisoner during Passover, would be omitted this year.

The prisoners were going to die to show the people who was in charge.

Martha and Eleazar crested the top of the Mount of Olive about an hour before sunset. There before them, across the Kidron Valley, was the beautiful Temple of God. It was gleaming in the evening sun. Normally, this was an awe inspiring sight, but not on this day. Martha felt the urgency of trying to locate Lois' friends' home. She knew they were close, so she prepared to start asking people who lived in the area where the home of Jonathan the Cheesemaker was? She felt a little uneasy asking for a stranger to extend to them hospitality, but if this didn't work, they would have to sleep, like many other pilgrims, under the stars on the Mount of Olives.

The first person Martha asked was a pleasant and helpful lady who smiled and proceeded to walk with her Galilean visitors a short distance. She soon pointed to a nice house and said, "That's where Jonathan the Cheesemaker, and his wife, Abigail live."

Martha thanked her profusely. The kind lady turned to walk away, while bidding them a Happy Passover. After dismounting from their wagon, Martha prompted Eleazar to knock on the door of the house. Within seconds, a robust man yanked the door open and greeted them. "Martha, Eleazar, please, please come in! Our home is your home. I'm Jonathan and this," turning to a lovely lady behind him, "is my darling wife, Abigail."

Martha's mouth was stuck open with disbelief. How could this stranger possibly know who they were? Both of the visitors were dumbfounded by this unusual greeting from Jonathan, like they were long lost, friends. When asked about how he knew them, both Jonathan and Abigail broke into laughter. Lois, who couldn't afford it, had made her way back over to Joshua of Gilboa, and paid him to send another carrier pigeon to Isaac in Jerusalem. Isaac had made it overnight to alert Jonathan and Abigail of Lois' message to please accept her two dear friends and extend hospitality to them. Without going into all the details, Lois asked them to offer a place for Martha and Eleazar to stay for a couple of days, as if they were offering that blessing to her. Jonathan and Abigail were happy to comply.

Especially since it was Passover time.

As the guests entered the lovely home, Abigail insisted they eat some food she had prepared. Jonathan had gone to the wagon to unhook the horses to feed and water them for the night. Their kindness and generosity was above and beyond anything Martha had ever experienced. The food was wonderful, and the home was beautiful. Eleazar thought, *I didn't know there was this much money in cheese.* Before Martha and Eleazar finished their food, Jonathan rejoined them. Martha offered to give them some money to pay for their expenses, but Abigail wouldn't hear of it. She said, "It's our honor and privilege to help you in this desperate time of need--in the name of the Lord."

Martha looked confused, "What do you mean, in the name of the Lord?"

Abigail continued as Jonathan smiled, "Well, we are disciples of Jesus and we call Him, Lord. We love helping people, we then share with them all the wonderful things Jesus has done for us."

Martha and Eleazar both smiled and she said, "We know what you mean. We, too, have had our experiences with Jesus. A while back we had wonderful fellowship with another disciple. Her name was Mary Magdalene. Do you know her?"

"No kidding" Abigail broadened her already big smile. "She's like a sister to me and she has stayed at our home many times when Jesus was in the area. In fact, Jesus has stayed here a couple of times when Lazarus of Bethany's house was too full."

"Wow," Eleazar couldn't contain his excitement. "Did He stay in the bed I'll be sleeping in tonight?"

"Yes, indeed," said Jonathan. "I think it's His favorite place to sleep."

They all laughed.

Jonathan continued, "We believe Jesus is the Son of God, and He has come to show us and teach us the ways of God. He says and does the miraculous, and we have been His followers for a couple of years, now. Jesus is God's promised Messiah, and we are proclaiming His name every chance we get."

"Amazing," said Eleazar. "Did you hear about Jesus raising the widow's son from the dead up in Nain?" Their hosts both nodded affirmatively. "Well, that was Lois' son, Philip. Mom and I were right there when Jesus raised him back to life. Philip is my best friend."

"No way," responded Jonathan, with a stunned look on his face. "Of course, we heard about that remarkable miracle, but we didn't know until this moment it was our friend Lois and Philip. Hallelujah and Praise the Lord! That is such a wonderful story. Abigail, did you hear that, it was Lois and Philip?"

"Yes, I was sitting right here," she laughed. "But I can't believe Lois hadn't shared that with us before now. I'm so glad you and your son were there to see that remarkable wonder. Did you hear about Jesus' most recent miracle of raising someone from the dead?"

"What? No!" said Martha.

"Yes, it happened just over the hill in Bethany a couple of days ago" Abigail answered. "Jesus was still up in Galilee when his close friend Lazarus suddenly got very sick. His sisters, Mary and Martha, sent word to Jesus to come quickly because of Lazarus' severe state. Before Jesus could arrive, Lazarus passed away, and everyone was grieving, especially his sisters. Four days after Lazarus died, Jesus and his disciples arrived, but all the people lamented He hadn't come sooner. Maybe Jesus could have cured him before he died."

"What did He do?" Eleazar asked.

"Well," Abigail continued with a smile on her face, "Jesus had the sisters and mourners escort Him out to the cemetery where Lazarus was entombed. A whole bunch of us were there when Jesus instructed that the stone that sealed the tomb should be rolled back. There were objections because after four days, the stench of decay would have been terrible, but at His word there were men who moved the stone back. We all watched in rapt attention, breathlessly wondering what Jesus was going to do. Suddenly, Jesus approached the opening and simply, but boldly said, 'Lazarus, come out!' A few seconds later, Lazarus came out, staggering under the restraints of his grave linens. Everyone just stood there in amazement. So Jesus commanded those standing around to remove Lazarus' wrappings and let him loose from his bindings. When Mary and Martha completed that task, there Lazarus stood, looking around and smiling, but not completely understanding what was happening. Suddenly he was being embraced by his sisters and the crowd of people started pressing toward him. There were those of us who were praising and glorifying God, all the while Jesus just stood there and smiled. It truly was amazing and the fame of Jesus spread like wildfire all around Jerusalem. But not everyone was happy."

"Who wouldn't be happy about a man rising from the dead?" asked Martha.

Jonathan fielded this question, "The religious leaders had already expressed their disdain for Jesus because He didn't present Himself to them first, and because He was stealing the loyalty of the people. They saw Jesus as a threat to their power and authority, so they determined He had to be removed. The raising of Lazarus was such a popular and amazing miracle, the Sadducees and Pharisees have been contriving on how they could eradicate Jesus from the scene in order to maintain their cozy relationship with the Romans and keep the power for themselves. Jesus was the main obstacle and threat to them, so now there's a plot to try and kill Jesus. Can you believe that?"

"What? No way?" said Eleazar. "Who would want to kill Jesus after all the good and noble things He has done? That doesn't make sense at all."

"You wouldn't think so," added Jonathan, "But when you're in power and you feel that control slipping away, you will do almost anything to maintain your grasp on supremacy. If you have to remove a threat because He is too perfect, then so be it!"

"That's unbelievable," responded Eleazar. "If Jesus *is* the Messiah, then He is the only hope for our nation--not the religious leaders. I sure hope Jesus escapes and gets somewhere safe."

Jonathan concluded, "He doesn't seem afraid of what they will do to Him. His name, Jesus, means Savior and that's why He has come to rescue and redeem us. What that will require, we don't know. But He does. With His miraculous power, I guess He could wipe them all out. That would be exciting to see, don't you think, Eleazar?"

"Absolutely!" was the best response Eleazar could muster.

After this, the discussion turned to Martha and her plans about Simeon.

CHAPTER FIFTEEN

A Zealot is Encouraged

MARTHA SUMMARIZED FOR Jonathan and Abigail what had happened resulting in Simeon's arrest and possible execution. Both of them winced as they heard the story. In the past, both Jonathan and Abigail had been touched by the brutality of the Romans. After hearing the teachings of Jesus though, they had genuinely tried to forgive their persecutors.

Martha wondered if they had any insights about whether or not the Romans would let family members see people being held at the Antonia jail. The next day would be Thursday, and Martha had a feeling things were going to escalate.

Jonathan was quick to respond, "I have never heard of the Romans cooperating with anyone about visiting prisoners. It's almost like they're happy to add that pain to the families awaiting the judgment of their loved ones. Have you heard anything different Abigail?"

"No, that's what I was going to say," she added.

"I just have to try," said Martha. "Maybe I can get a note to Simeon if they won't let us see him. I just want him to know we are here and that we will never forsake him."

"I'll be happy to take you and Eleazar over to the fortress tomorrow, and we'll see what happens. Maybe God will do something unusual for you," Jonathan said, trying to reassure them. With that, they all went to bed.

Knowing how desperate things were getting, both Martha and Eleazar once again slept restlessly. Each time Martha would twitch out of a light sleep, she would whisper a prayer, "Oh, Dear Jehovah, Please give Simeon your peace and rest. Help him to not be afraid as he 'walks through the Valley of the Shadow of Death.' God, please do not let him be tortured or abused." And for the first time Martha prayed, "Father, Let us be able to follow the teachings of Jesus, and be willing to forgive Simeon's tormentors, too. Amen." After praying that prayer multiple times through the night, she finally felt a calming peace, one that allowed her to sleep for several hours just before dawn. The next morning, Abigail prepared a special breakfast of eggs, meat, bread, and multiple fruits--with milk and water to drink. Martha and Eleazar hadn't eaten like that for many days. It was wonderfully refreshing.

There was also plenty of cheese.

Following breakfast, Martha expressed concern about going over to Antonia. She didn't want Jonathan or Abigail to be associated with a family of troublemakers. She was also worried about Jonathan missing work. Jonathan quickly assured her he wasn't working because it was Passover Week and they were approaching the high, holy, Sabbath. Therefore, their shop was closed, and they had nothing better to do than accompany Martha and Eleazar over to the pavement outside of Antonia. After making preparations, they all went to the Roman fortress.

Their path took them down the slopes of the Mount of Olives, and toward the Temple complex which was across the Kidron Valley. As they descended the mount, they noticed travelers and pilgrims camped out all over the side of the hill. Martha knew that's where she and Eleazar would have camped if not for the hospitality of Jonathan and Abigail. As they reached the valley, Martha was puzzled by something she had never seen before, so she asked Jonathan a question.

"Why is the water of this stream running red in color?"

"Oh," Jonathan responded, "For many years now, there have been so many people coming to Jerusalem and the Temple at Passover time, to worship God and offer sin offerings, or trespass offerings, or thanksgiving offerings, the Temple priests had to create a way of cleaning off the altars. They use so much water to flush off all the blood residue, it flows down the back side of the Kidron slopes outside the Eastern Gate, and it ends up here in the Kidron Brook. For years now, during Passover Week, the Kidron Brook will run red with the blood of animal sacrifices. That's what you're seeing today."

"Oh, wow," was Martha's reply. "I've never seen that before."

They continued up the hillside to some steps that led them through the Eastern Gate and into the Temple compound. Even at this early hour, there was a huge throng of people. In fact, Martha never remembered seeing so many people on any of her many previous visits to the Temple. She noticed all of the vendors who were hawking their goods. Both she and Eleazar marveled at the many groups of Rabbis teaching their students about the Law and the Prophets.

They overheard many of them rehearsing the story from Exodus about the night in Egypt when God required the Israelites to offer a lamb, and put its blood on the two doorposts of the entrance to their houses, and overhead on the beam above the doorways. This act of obedience to God allowed the people inside to be spared when God sent the tenth plague throughout Egypt. Every eldest son in a household who was under the protection of the blood of the lamb, was spared when God sent the "Death Angel" to go throughout the country. Anyone who did not follow God's command to place the blood on the doorway, suffered the judgment of God when the eldest son in that house, unprotected by the blood covering, died at the coming of the Angel. This consequence affected everyone, right up to the household of Pharaoh. This is the reason the Jews had been celebrating the Passover for 1,500 years.

Jonathan and Abigail said it was a common thing for Jesus to come to this area called, "Solomon's Porch," to teach and preach to His growing number of disciples. On many occasions they had come to be under His instruction and tutelage. Every time they heard Jesus speak, they believed they were hearing the Words from God, Himself.

And they were!

As they looked around on this Thursday morning, they were disappointed they did not see Him on this day. Maybe He would come later. As they passed by the Temple, Martha never remembered seeing it this beautiful. This was one of the most wonderful temples in the whole world, and it was dedicated to the God of Israel.

But the hustle and bustle of the crowds seemed to emphasize a lack of worshipful attitudes. In fact, Martha noticed this time, and pointed it out to Eleazar, how many people were coming through the Eastern Gate, passing right by the Temple of God without noticing it, and hastily walking out the gate on the western side that entered into the city of Jerusalem. They were using this pathway by the Temple as a shortcut into the city so they didn't have to walk around the walls. How pitiful, she thought, that they had reduced God's holy, house, into a walkway to shorten their trip to and from the city.

Surely, this did not please God.

Jonathan continued leading their small group, and after taking some time to marvel at the sights, they exited on the west side of the Temple compound and into the city. Looming just a short distance to their right, heading north, was the impressive and imposing edifice of Antonia. This is where the Romans garrisoned while in Jerusalem in order to watch over the activities going on during Passover at the Temple. They believed that if any insurrections or riots were going to start, it would be here at the Temple. So they kept constant watch.

In fact, there were Roman soldiers watching as a group of four people walked directly over to the main entrance to the fortress. Most Jews didn't dare venture over this far. The milling soldiers outside of Antonia also took notice of this unusual circumstance and they stopped visiting and started staring. Jonathan approached one soldier who seemed to be in a special uniform and politely asked if he spoke Hebrew. He indicated that he did, but just a little bit. Jonathan asked if he was in command here or could he speak with someone in authority. The Roman guard kindly indicated for Jonathan to wait and he would find someone who could communicate better. He returned shortly with a soldier who was even more impressively decorated. The Roman, in very good Hebrew, introduced himself as, "Markus, the Centurion."

Jonathan introduced himself and then asked permission for Martha to speak to the Centurion. Markus nodded and Martha walked over to the kind-looking man.

"My name is Martha, and my son and I are from Cana of Galilee," she started. In her heart, she was praying, "Oh, God, please direct every word I say." Then she continued to address Markus. "My son, Eleazar, and I have come all this way to ask of you a very unusual request. We have been told that my husband, Simeon the Stone Mason, is being held here facing a sentence of crucifixion. I know it is probably impossible, but is there any way my son and I can visit with him for just a moment, and express to him our love and prayers?"

Markus didn't immediately respond but then deliberately said, "Martha, I am sorry but visitors are strictly forbidden here. What is your husband accused of doing?"

Tentatively, Martha answered, "Sir, I'm not exactly sure. I believe he was forced to participate in a robbery, I think, in Jericho. But I am unaware of what happened, except that he ended up here."

Markus now understood the incident and the participants and said, "Ma'am, your husband was arrested because he was part of a plot to steal from the Roman Empire. Other than being a participant in the failed attempt, he was apprehended while helping a more notorious criminal, a man named, Barabbas, who we believe has committed murders trying to incite insurrections."

Martha thought it best that she not volunteer that Barabbas was her cousin.

She interrupted, "Sir, I know you are a man of great authority. I believe God has allowed me to visit with you personally so that I might get a special dispensation to let me see Simeon and talk briefly to him. Would you please allow my son and me to see him?"

Markus, understanding her passionate appeal, thought for a moment and then answered, "Martha, it is impossible for any Jews to enter into Antonia, unless we bring a prisoner to this place. I will, however, let you write a note to your husband, and I will assure you that he will receive it, because I will personally deliver it to him. But that is all I can do, and I might get into trouble for doing that."

Martha quickly said, "Oh, thank you sir, can I have just a moment to write the note?"

Markus nodded affirmatively, and even handed her a parchment and quill with an ink pot. Martha thought, *God directed me to this special man to help me.* She eagerly accepted his gift and this opportunity to write Simeon a brief letter. Now, what could she possibly say to him?

Martha began to compose:

My dearest husband, I love you more than anything in this world. I came to Jerusalem, with Eleazar, hoping to see you, but that is not possible today. So accept my heartfelt letter this kind Roman official has allowed me to write. We know God is in control of all things and we accept His will. Our prayer is that you will be delivered back to us. But above everything else, we want you to know our love for you is eternal, and we will never forget you. You are the best man in the world and we are so blessed that you are my husband, and our children's father. No matter what happens, keep believing in God. Somehow, I just know Jesus is going to help see you through this ordeal. We are going to continue to try and see you! We love you forever, Martha, Eleazar, Lydia and John

With that, Martha let the scroll dry, and then rolled it up before handing it to Markus. Then spontaneously, she embraced him and, as if the words were guided by someone else, she said, "Thank you so much! May Jesus bless you for what you have done!" Even Martha seemed surprised at her choice of words.

Markus smiled uneasily as he tucked the parchment into his breastplate. Then he snapped off an about-face and regally walked away.

As the group turned to leave, Jonathan was the first to say something. "I can't believe what I just saw. I've never seen a Roman willing to help a Jew, especially a woman." Then turning to Martha, he said, "No offense." She smiled back at him. Then he continued, "I started getting fearful that not only was this a hopeless attempt, but maybe we could get in trouble for even trying."

Abigail chimed in, "Me too. When that first soldier walked away to get Markus, I really thought maybe he was going to bring back other guards to harass us."

Eleazar had the most insightful comment, "I think God made sure we had the chance to talk to Markus. I doubt any other soldier in the Roman Empire would have treated us with such kindness and offer a solution to allow Mom to write a letter to Abba. That was amazing."

Everyone agreed.

Although the outcome was less than they had
dreamed, it was more than they had honestly expected. As
they walked back to Jonathan and Abigail's house, all of
them believed Markus would fulfill his promise to get that
scroll to Simeon. Martha privately hoped she had said the
right things and that it would encourage her husband, even
though things looked so bleak.

Simeon, couldn't stop weeping after receiving the message
from Martha and Eleazar. He was momentarily fearful
when a ranking officer showed up at his cell door. *Oh no,*
he thought, *this can't be good.* Then he was shocked to
hear the Roman say in perfect Hebrew, this is from your
wife and son, handing him a parchment. With that, he
turned and walked away. Simeon, with a shaking hand,
unfurled the scroll to read his loving wife's script.

After reading the brief letter, he slumped to the floor
in tears, rejoicing that he had heard from someone--
especially them. He read the note over and over,
announcing through the prison bars to his condemned
partners what had happened. Of course, they wanted to
hear the message. Simeon reserved some of the private
comments for his knowledge only. The others commented
specifically about the line where Martha said, "Somehow,
I just know Jesus is going to help see you through this
ordeal." They wanted to know what that meant. So did
Simeon. He held tightly the letter as if it was the most
precious thing he owned.

At that moment it was.

That evening at Jonathan's house, Martha and Eleazar
joined with Abigail and Jonathan in the Passover Meal.
Earlier in the week, these loving disciples of Jesus had gone

and offered their own lamb as a sacrifice to God. Now, they all commemorated the memory of God's blessings upon the Children of Israel. Oh, they each hoped, if God could just make one more miracle happen, this time in the life of Simeon.

CHAPTER SIXTEEN

A Zealot is Freed

THAT FRIDAY MORNING the guests were once again greeted by the aroma of a generous breakfast being prepared by Abigail. They had completed their meal, and were beginning to clean up, when suddenly there was loud knocking on the front door. Jonathan and Abigail glanced at each other. He made his way over and opened the door. The sounds of several passionate men talking were heard, although the actual words were undetectable. After a moment, Jonathan came back with a sullen look on his face. "Abigail," he began, "They arrested Jesus last night and have taken Him before the Sanhedrin illegally with a nighttime trial."

Martha and Eleazar stared in disbelief.

"Why?" Abigail wanted to know. "What has He done to be arrested? And who are they?"

"Well, I don't know much," said Jonathan, "but apparently, the Chief Priests and Pharisees took many soldiers, Temple guards, and Romans who were afraid it could turn into a riot, when they went to the Garden of Gethsemane and arrested the Lord. I can't believe it myself, but they said Judas Iscariot was the one who pointed them to Jesus, in an act of betrayal."

"What?" blurted Abigail. "Judas was one of Jesus' close friends. How can this be happening? What are they doing with Jesus?"

Jonathan continued, "My friends said, after Caiaphas pronounced Jesus guilty of blasphemy, a quorum of the Sanhedrin found Him guilty and worthy of death. But now they have taken Him over to Antonia, because they have to get Pilate's permission before they can execute Jesus. Pilate won't say yes to a charge of blasphemy, he doesn't care about the Jewish justice system, so they have accused Jesus of insurrection—that He claimed to be the King."

"What can we do?" asked Abigail.

"Well," said Jonathan, "We're heading over that way to see what's happening with Simeon. Let's go right now and find out what they are doing to Jesus!"

Everyone headed over to the Fortress. They reviewed the matter over and over again, based on the limited details they had. They also wondered if these events were going to somehow affect Simeon. When they approached the legal *Bema Seat* of Pilate, a huge crowd had gathered, but most of them seemed to be siding with Caiaphas and the Sanhedrin. Very few of Jesus' followers were even aware of what was happening.

When the party arrived they found some friends who briefed them on what had happened up to that moment.

Pilate had interviewed Jesus and came out and said, "I find no fault in this man!" But the religious leaders kept things stirred up and then Pilate heard, again, that Jesus was from Nazareth, and therefore, a Galilean. Hoping to avoid this growing controversy, he decided to send Jesus over to Herod Antipas, the Tetrarch of Galilee, who was in town for the Passover.

So they took Jesus to Antipas up the hill to Herod the Great's old palace. He acknowledged that he didn't have the authority to execute Jesus, so he sent Him back to Pilate. Jesus and all His guards returned and the Jewish leaders explained Herod Antipas' position to Pilate. Now, Pilate *had* to make a decision.

They all tried to move in closer to hear what was being said.

Inside the jailhouse in Antonia, a commotion could be detected by Simeon and the others, but they had no idea what was happening. The guards had been scurrying around all morning, and they had shared enough details with the prisoners to let them know something big was going on outside. Some of the Roman soldiers had been a part of those activities. Barabbas concluded the noise was probably a large group of Zealots who were coming to release the three freedom fighters from prison. But Simeon didn't believe that at all.

Occasionally, the men were able to make out a few faint words from outside, but the bulk of the dialogue was indiscernible. Even though the three assumed today was going bring calamity for them, maybe these events outside were changing things.

Earlier in the week, Pontius Pilate had determined there was going to be a crucifixion today so that he could assert his dominance over the Jews during their Passover celebrations. He had also earlier determined that he was going to skip the traditional releasing of a prisoner, an annual act designed to appease the Jewish masses. But since this Jesus dilemma had emerged, he was scrambling trying to figure out a way to let Jesus go. Pilate was convinced Jesus was not guilty of insurrection, but he was trying to save face with the Jews by releasing Him, while showing he was still in control.

So Pilate decided he would give them an option of who they wanted to be released from custody that day. Pilate seemed rather pleased with himself as he prepared to extend this olive branch to the people, because he was totally confident the masses would cry out for Jesus of Nazareth to be released. In order to make the choice even more obvious in Jesus' favor, Pilate decided to offer a notorious criminal named Barabbas, someone he was certain would be rejected because of his evil life.

The man was a murderer.

Pilate emerged after Jesus returned from Herod Antipas' palace. He felt bad that he had placed such a burden on Antipas, even though they were not all that close to each other. Now, both of them had this *Jesus problem* to commiserate over how to handle it. Pilate just knew his strategy was going to work. So he hushed the crowd and in regal tones said, "Annually, here at Passover, I have observed a custom for you Jews. I want to show you how magnanimous and thoughtful I am towards you by continuing this tradition again this year. I am going to release to you someone who has been arrested, and I'm going to pardon this criminal."

When she heard those words, Martha suddenly remembered her wish from several days earlier, that maybe Simeon would be the beneficiary of such judicial forgiveness. Is it possible Simeon might be the candidate

Pilate proposes as an option for this salvation? She hoped with all her heart it would be her husband!

Pontius Pilate had Jesus of Nazareth brought before the crowd. Then without physically bringing forward another candidate for the people to consider, Pilate gave them the contenders to choose from for deliverance. Again, Pilate hushed the crowd and announced the two options. "Who do you want me to release from custody, Jesus of Nazareth?"

Martha and Eleazar's heart skipped a beat hoping Simeon would be announced. But then, he would have to be going against Jesus. Oh, no!

Pilate now gave the other option, "Or do you want me to release to you, Jesus Barabbas?" Pilate paused to let the crowd respond.

Martha was disappointed upon hearing the options. Barabbas? Really? Yes, he was her cousin, but he had done some wicked things. She didn't know them all but she knew enough. Barabbas shouldn't be released over Jesus.

The Chief Priests and officers of the Sanhedrin had been manipulating the crowd and inciting them to all cry out against Jesus. So when Pilate proposed the two choices, he was shocked when the crowd started yelling, "Barabbas! Barabbas!"

In the jail, the chant of the crowd outside started becoming very distinct. It was loud enough to clearly hear as the three prisoners heard the cries of, "Barabbas! Barabbas!" Any other accompanying words could not be discerned. But all three men immediately perked up when hearing one of their group being called out.

Pilate was in shock when he heard the crowd's choice. Little did he know the Jewish leaders had whipped them up into a frenzy. Staggered by this, Pilate had a follow-up question that only those in front of him could hear. The prisoners would not have been able to understand Pilate's query from their distance. Pilate's follow up was, "What should I do with Jesus?" Pilate couldn't believe his ears when he, as well as Barabbas, heard the words, "Let Him be crucified! Crucify Him!"

Barabbas was stunned by what appeared to be happening. All he could make out from his prison cell was, "Barabbas," and "Crucify him!" He had believed his exploits would have been appreciated and applauded by the bulk of the Jewish people. He was a real patriot and for them to now clamor for his crucifixion was a terrible blow. Now, he awaited what he believed would be the death penalty.

Sure enough, before long the Roman soldiers came, rousted all three men, and opened their cell doors. It now appeared that all three of them, including Simeon, were on their way to an excruciating death.

Outside, Pilate hoped that by scourging Jesus maybe the crowd would be assuaged and agree to His release. But even after beating Him mercilessly, the Jewish leaders still demanded Pilate follow through with the execution. Since the Roman mode of demise was the only option, Jesus was heading to death on a Cross.

Pilate finally capitulated to the Jewish religious authorities and reluctantly agreed to Jesus' execution. In one final act of avoidance, he took a basin of water and washed his hands of the blood of the innocent man.

When the three Zealots came out of the prison, they saw sunlight for the first time in many days. They squinted and tried to focus on their surroundings. When they could finally see clearly, they stared at the three death instruments--the newly created crosses. Simeon and Micah were instructed to go and pick up their crosses, which they would carry to Golgotha, "the Place of the Skull," where crucifixions were carried out.

But to everyone's surprise, Barabbas was ushered over to the exit door of Antonia and told he was free to go. He had been pardoned. Not only was he flabbergasted, having been certain of his imminent death, but his two compatriots, who were only involved in the crime of stealing, were condemned to die. The whole thing was baffling. But Barabbas slowly slipped out of his confinement and into his new-found freedom. The third cross, the one that had been built for Barabbas, was delivered to Jesus by the Roman soldiers, and He was forced to carry it, as well, even in His emaciated condition.

Barabbas soon discovered what had transpired in the "Pavement," the judgment seat of Pilate. He was awestruck by the outcome. He was certain he was about to die, but now Jesus was going to die on the cross that had been prepared for him. These changes to his destiny certainly made him think.

The two thieves were led away before the guards took Jesus. They exited out a back gate, but Martha and Eleazar were told about their pathway, so they gave chase, trying to catch up with Simeon. Jonathan and Abigail joined the group of Jesus' disciples who were following Him to the death hill. As they approached the small mount the Romans called *Calvary*, Martha and Eleazar were able to find, and walk alongside Simeon. The Roman soldiers had pity on them and let them talk and weep together. Simeon, in complete shock, still snapped back to a moment of joy when his wife and son caught up with him. He was so happy to see them, but he was also humiliated for them to see what was going to become of him.

Eleazar offered, and the Roman soldiers allowed him to help carry his father's cross. Going a different route to Calvary, Jesus also needed help with His Cross, and a pilgrim by the name of Simon the Cyrenian assisted the Lord with His burden.

CHAPTER SEVENTEEN

A Zealot is Redeemed

AT GOLGOTHA, KNOWN to the locals as *the place of the skull*, the executioners began the process of crucifying the two thieves. They were experts at their craft. They laid the crosses on the ground and started to position the criminals on their individual death bier. For a fleeting moment, the guard allowed Simeon a chance to hug his wife and son one more time. The embrace was vice-like as Simeon knew he was facing the end of his life and would never again experience this circle of love.

Finally, the soldier separated them, as Martha stole one more kiss. Simeon instructed Eleazar to be the man of the house when he was gone. By this time, Micah, who had no family or friends around, was receiving the death blows as they bound him to his cross. His shrieks of pain frightened Simeon who knew it was now his time. Micah recoiled with every hammer blow upon the nails in his hands and feet. He also threatened and swore oaths that he would kill every one of his persecutors if he ever had a chance.

Simeon prayed to Jehovah for grace. He didn't want to react in a similar way in front of his wife and son. He wanted to do his best not to do or say anything that would be disgraceful and leave that image in his family's mind. But now it was his moment.

The Roman soldier who had primarily ushered Simeon to this hill of death had been rather kind, allowing him to walk with Martha and Eleazar, even letting the young man help carry his Abba's cross. It was unheard of that they would let a family have a moment to share final thoughts of love. Usually, the mistreatment was just another part of the persecution and torture they wanted to inflict. Simeon recognized that his executioner had been one of the guards who watched over him in the prison.

Little did he know, the guard had been able to pick up portions of dialogue between Simeon and his other saboteurs. Along the way, the Roman had ascertained that Simeon was only a pawn, and it was Barabbas who was the main perpetrator and murderer. So this guard had grown a little soft-hearted towards Simeon and even a little angry at the fact the Prefect let Barabbas go.

So, as he was ready to position Simeon on his instrument of martyrdom, he had him drink some vinegar-wine mixed with myrrh. He whispered to Simeon that it would help dull the pain a little, because now the soldier's duty would no longer let him be kind. As Simeon, doing his best to be strong, lay down on the cross, he stretched out his arms, exposing his open hands. Glancing quickly in

Micah's direction, he saw hateful stares and he heard agonizing screams, as the Romans had finished nailing him to his cross and were wrapping ropes around his wrists to help support his weight once they elevated him and then dropped it in the hole they had previously carved into the bedrock.

Just before the first blow of the hammer, Simeon shifted his gaze to the people he loved. As Martha and Eleazar, who had been forced back a little from the scene, stared in disbelief and horror, they were wiping away the steady stream of tears. Simeon thought how much he loved them all! His Roman executioner was about to strike the first blow when Simeon caught the scent of newly carved wood. It was coming from his cross. The first piercing nail fired through his wrist with such intensity, Simeon instinctively moaned, but he didn't yell. Several more shocks of the hammer resulted in the same guttural noises. The pain was so overwhelming, he thought he was about to blackout.

That would have been a blessing.

Moving to the other hand, his guard sympathetically poured some vinegar-wine with the myrrh on his forearm and hand. By this time some of the soldiers who had finished with Micah and dropped his cross in the hole that held it firmly in place, had moved over to assist with Simeon. They stationed themselves by his feet and forcefully crossed his left foot on top of his right one.

There was a small jutting piece of wood on which his feet were resting. As he watched all of these activities, the first nail ripped through his right wrist. The pain again staggered him, and he let out an uncontrollable cry. Almost instantaneously, the other soldiers started driving the nails in his feet, tying him to the cross. As much as his hands caused him to scream in pain, his feet were even worse.

Again, an involuntary shriek forced its way out of his lungs. Alternating between the hammer hitting his hands and his feet, the fiery pain was overwhelming.

Suddenly, God gave Simeon some momentary relief as he slumped into unconsciousness. The soldiers completed their tasks with only reflexive groans from Simeon. Martha and Eleazar turned away from the scene before them. Martha was certain that with every strike of the nails, she was feeling piercing in her heart.

Before Simeon regained consciousness, the group with Jesus arrived. Martha and Eleazar glanced in His direction and could hardly believe their eyes. Jesus had been so badly beaten and brutalized. He was bleeding from His face and His back and almost didn't appear human. It was terrible. Simon, the bearer of Jesus' Cross for the last portion of their trek, laid it down where the Romans instructed. He positioned it near another waiting hole. Those in the entourage accompanying Jesus were crying and praying as their Lord tried to reassure them everything was all right.

Martha saw Jonathan and Abigail in the crowd. Then she noticed Mary Magdalene, the woman who had testified about Jesus to her and Lois in Nain. Then Martha saw Mary, the mother of Jesus. She was the one who had so tenderly spoken about Jesus at the wedding in Cana. Now, she was emotionally drained, and her pain was evident on her face. Only a mother or wife could commiserate about such an event. Martha thought it was about to get worse.

When they started to nail Jesus to that cursed cross.

At that moment, Martha's attention was redirected by Eleazar toward the Romans lifting Simeon up on his cross and dropping him with a thud into the carved hole. Still unconscious, Simeon moaned. Martha was so glad he had blacked out prior to the last blows from his executioners. She noticed he was starting to wake. As she stared in his direction, she saw, for the first time, a placard over the main beam of Simeon's cross and above his head.

There was only one word, written in Hebrew, Greek, and Latin-- *THIEF.*

The Romans wanted anyone who could read to be able to interpret one of these three universal languages and know the crime for which this person was being crucified. They wanted every crucifixion to be a bold declaration of the crimes that were worthy of death. Their hope was that crucifixions would be a deterrent to anyone who might consider violating the laws of the Roman Empire.

Jesus was now on the cross, still wearing on a cluster of thorns on his forehead, one that had been fashioned into a mock crown. He had calmly and voluntarily laid down and stretched out His arms, even though His bleeding back fired up raw nerves throughout His body. He went through the same process as Simeon, but there seemed to be a difference. Though Jesus flinched and winced with each blow, He maintained a calm, almost angelic demeanor. He was strong and meek at the same time. He never cried out or railed against any of His tormentors. While most people in the crowd cried and shrieked, Jesus accepted the wrath of the Roman soldiers and never lashed out at them, the way Micah had done.

Simeon didn't either, now that Martha thought about it, but his lack of awareness helped him through the ordeal. But Jesus never lost consciousness. After weathering the storm of the Roman death merchants, He was bound by ropes around His wrist and forearms, holding Him to the crossbeam.

When they started raising Jesus up, everyone in the crowd cried and some turned away. As Jesus was raised up between heaven and earth, His cross slid into its sleeve with a loud thud. It even seemed to shake the ground. Jesus involuntarily groaned as most of His disciples gasped at the horror before them. There was Jesus, hanging between two thieves. Micah was hanging to His left and Simeon to His right. Jesus looked at the criminals as if praying for them. It was at that moment, Martha noticed the placard above Jesus' head.

It read, again in three languages: *JESUS OF NAZARETH THE KING OF THE JEWS.*

Martha looked at His mother, Mary, who was buckling at the scene that was unfolding before her. Mary Magdalene and a couple of other women, with one man also with them, tried to comfort her. But she was inconsolable.

It was at that moment that Martha recognized another figure in the crowd. Off to the side was a military man in full battle array. But Martha knew she had seen him before. She turned to Eleazar and asked him, "Who is that Roman Officer over there?"

It only took Eleazar a second to remember his name. "That is Markus, the Roman Centurion who helped us smuggle the parchment to father yesterday," Eleazar responded.

"Yes! That's who it is," Martha said. "It was so nice of him to help us. I had no idea he was the supervisor for all these crucifixions. What an awful job to have."

Martha again set her gaze on Simeon.

Crucifixion is a painful, torturous, mode of punishment that literally causes the victim to smother to death. When those being crucified find it difficult to breathe, they are forced to pull up against the nails in their hands and push up against the nails in their feet. As painful as that is, it gives a momentary opportunity to breathe in some much-needed clean air. But they can only sustain that rhythm for a few seconds before slumping back down to get some relief from the excruciating pain in their extremities.

Back and forth this motion goes, and that's the pattern Simeon and the others found themselves following. Because there was so little air in their lungs, speaking was very difficult. So, Simeon had said few words. Micah actually mustered up enough strength to rail against Jesus, belittling Him and challenging Him to take them all down from the cross. Initially, even Simeon encouraged Jesus to take some action to help them all. Everyone knew He had worked all of those miracles, why not one more for them?

Jesus' first words were radically different. After His tormentors finished pinioning the victims to a cross, they just sat down and stared at the malefactors. Some gambled over His clothes in fulfillment of Hebrew prophecy. So when Jesus spoke, His words were shocking. Lifting up on the Cross so He could breathe, Jesus cried out in a strong and forceful voice, speaking about those who had just nailed Him to the Cross, *"Father, forgive them, they don't know what they are doing!"* Heads snapped up as Jesus spoke those most amazing words of forgiveness. Simeon and Micah took notice.

Consider this truth: the people God forgives, they go to Heaven. Now, Jesus wasn't asking God to take all these sinners to Heaven, but He was willing to see them come to a point where they too could experience the grace of God and become His children. It was truly remarkable.

Jesus spoke words of comfort to His mother, who was positioned at the foot of the cross. He gave instructions to His beloved friend, John the Disciple, to take care of Mary after He was gone. Interestingly, Jesus had several half-brothers (same mother, different Father). According to Jewish culture, they should have assumed the mantle of taking care of their mother. But apparently all of Jesus' brethren were still in unbelief. So, Jesus wanted John to promise he would watch out for Mary.

By this point, Martha and Eleazar had positioned themselves in front of Simeon. Mary Magdalene, and Mary the mother of Jesus, had both acknowledged her as they remembered their previous encounters. Now all of them were involved in the most painful moment of their lives. Martha was staring up at Simeon with a broken heart, as he tried to force a smile in her direction between gasps for breath. All the while, he reflected on the gracious words he had just heard from the lips of Jesus. Never had he seen such compassion toward an enemy as what Jesus expressed to those soldiers. The words to His mother were also so selfless and loving. All of a sudden from the other side of Jesus, Micah again began to blast words at Jesus saying, *"If you are really the Christ, save yourself and us!"*

Realizing the words came from his co-conspirator, Simeon pulled himself up and looking past Jesus said directly to Micah, *"Don't you fear God, seeing that you are also condemned and about to enter eternity?"* Simeon drew in some more air and continued, *" We are here justly because of the sins we committed. But Jesus has never done anything wrong!"*

Martha and Eleazar hung on every word Simeon was saying.

Then Simeon turned to Jesus and mustered all the strength he could and said, *"Jesus, Lord, remember me when you come into your kingdom!"* This was not a cry for deliverance, but a plea for redemption and salvation. Simeon, after hearing all the stories about Jesus, now had witnessed firsthand the actions of Deity. He believed that Jesus was the Lord. He accepted what the name Jesus literally meant, *Savior.* He agreed with Eleazar's conclusion many months earlier, after seeing Philip resurrected back to life by Jesus, "He really is God!"

Simeon was ready to trust Jesus with his eternal soul.

Jesus forced a kind smile in the direction of his new brother. Then He said to Simeon, *"Truly, I want you to know, because of your faith, today you will be with me in Paradise!"* What a precious promise of Simeon's eternal destiny. Martha, Eleazar, Jonathan, Abigail, Mary Magdalene, John the Disciple, and Jesus' mother, Mary, all heard these words of promise and salvation. Simeon had come to this moment as a condemned Zealot, but he was leaving this life as a redeemed child of God. Hallelujah!

Martha and Eleazar particularly reveled in the newfound life Simeon experienced through the promise of Jesus. They too wanted to embrace this same offer of eternity with Jesus and a reunion with Simeon. They now knew because of what Jesus was doing at this moment in time, all people would be candidates for redemption and salvation if they would follow Simeon's lead and admit they were sinners and justifiably condemned. After admitting that fallen condition, all they needed to do was call upon the name of Jesus to be saved. Simeon immediately realized the new life and hope that had been imparted to him by Jesus. He was forever changed. He knew these last fleeting moments of life were but a light affliction compared to the eternal joy with Jesus that awaited him. In the midst of one of the horrors of crucifixion, eternal life was born because of Jesus' amazing grace.

Soon after Simeon's redemption was completed, a most unusual phenomenon took place. At about noon, a gloomy, piercing, eerie, darkness chased away the sun, blocking its life-giving rays. Everyone felt the blackness of night in the middle of the day. This was an ominous, if not devilish, circumstance--a foreboding sign to all who witnessed it. The gloomy transformation was certainly tied to the crucifixion of these three men, especially Jesus. It lasted until 3:00 pm, when the Lamb of God became the ultimate, perfect sacrifice. Markus, the centurion who was supervising all of the day's events, realized this crucifixion was unlike any other he had ever witnessed.

Jesus made a few more statements while hanging on His Cross. The most impactful and disconcerting was when, near the end of His life, Jesus cried out with a loud voice that silenced everyone around, *"My God, My God, why have you forsaken me?"* The human observers did not fully grasp the profound nature of that moment in history. God the Father, who was unable to look upon Sin, had to turn away from His beloved Son, because Jesus had taken upon Himself all the sins of the world in order to accept God's wrath and judgment upon Sin.

For Jesus to truly provide redemption for everyone, not just Simeon, He had to die and His blood had to eternally accomplish what the yearly sacrifice of a lamb by the High Priest did for the people on Yom Kippur-- atonement. Jesus' death and sacrifice covered the sins of the whole world so that God would accept Jesus' payment for the sins of all mankind. But in that moment in time while He was on the Cross, Jesus understood His Father had turned away because He could not behold sin. Jesus gave everything in order to pay for our redemption.

A short time later, as Simeon continued to struggle, and as the onlookers winced with his every agonizing breath, and with Micah who still seemed defiant to the bitter end, Jesus said His last words. Everyone stood up and listened as Jesus prepared his final statement. Jesus breathed in a deep breath as He said, loudly, in the Greek language, "*TETELESTAI*," which means, *It is Finished!* Then He continued, *"Father, into your hands, I yield My Spirit!"*

After acknowledging He had done everything required to satisfy the Father's righteous justice against Sin, Jesus bowed His head and surrendered His Spirit. He was in control right up to the last moment of His earthly life. Simeon turned his head away from Jesus and began to cry.

Jesus's mother wept bitterly, as if her own heart had been pierced, while John tried to console her. Mary Magdalene, Martha, and Eleazar all had tears streaming down their face. They couldn't believe this perfect man had died. Martha redirected her gaze back to Simeon, who was still weeping. Their eyes met and Simeon forced out a smile. Then in hushed tones that only she and Eleazar could hear from their vantage point at the bottom of his cross, Simeon pushed out, "I will be with Jesus soon. And all of us will one day be together because of Him." With that Simeon writhed in pain and slumped, putting his weight on his already agonizing extremities.

At the exact moment of Jesus' death, the earth shook as if it was revolting at the fact its Creator had died. All those beholding the event had to associate this phenomenon with the passing of Jesus. But the most hard-hearted in the crowd were glad to see this faux Messiah finally gone. Maybe now things would get back to normal. The religious leaders were eager to re-establish their dominance over the people again. Now, these same Jewish authorities appealed to Pontius Pilate one more time. They pointed out this Friday evening was a special Sabbath. It was a high, holy, Sabbath because it coincided with the Passover. Therefore, they didn't want any of those malefactors hanging on crosses during this Holy Day, which would begin at sunset. Could Pilate please hasten their deaths and get them off those crosses? Pilate, acquiescing to the Jewish aristocrats, agreed to those terms.

After the earthquake in the wake of Jesus' death, Martha overheard Markus the Centurion say, as though talking to himself, *"Truly this man was the Son of God!"* He had walked closer to those around the crosses, but most people had not noticed. Since he now stood quite close to them, Martha heard his declaration.

Coming from a place of strength she did not know she had, Martha asked him, "Are you a follower of Jesus?" Markus was somewhat surprised at the question. Thoughtfully and deliberately, and as Simeon and Eleazar watched on, Markus shared his brief story in hushed tones, so that only the three of them could hear him. He said, "I have known Jesus for some time and have come to believe He is the Messiah of the Jews. Today's events just solidified my firm belief that He is God's Son. About a year ago, I was stationed up in the Galilee and I met Jesus in Capernaum. I sought Him out. I had a close friend, a servant in my household I considered as a son. He was gravely ill and about to die. I had heard of this Nazarene miracle worker and so I approached Jesus and asked if He would heal my servant? Jesus was prepared to come to my house, and I said He didn't need to come. I believed He had the authority and power to heal my servant from there in Capernaum. He acknowledged my faith and said, 'He's healed.' I had started back to my home wondering what I would find with my friend, and another person from my household met me on the road to tell me my servant had made a full recovery. He was healed. From that time on I have believed Jesus was supernatural and He had been sent by God. Everything that happened today has confirmed that belief in my heart and mind. But today, I acknowledged He truly was God's Son, and the very essence of God, Himself."

Martha, Simeon, and Eleazar listened to this story with rapt attention. They once again thanked Markus for the kindnesses he had shown to them. They now knew it was because he had a relationship with Jesus.

Markus smiled in appreciation for their kind words. At that moment another soldier walked up to Markus and gave him a message from Pontius Pilate. He nodded affirmatively. Then he turned to Martha and Eleazar and apologized for what he had to do next. He explained that he had been ordered to hasten the deaths of Simeon and Micah by breaking their legs. This painful outcome would mean the men on the cross would be unable to support themselves and breathe.

Death would follow shortly thereafter.

As the soldiers prepared to deliver these death strokes, Martha looked at Simeon and loudly declared her love for him. Simeon tried to prepare himself for the trauma that was about to be inflicted upon him. He raised up on his cramping feet so he could make one more statement of undying love for all of them. He held his breath as the Roman soldiers took mallets and smashed them against his thigh bones. Instinctively, he yelled in pain as every nerve ending in his body seemed to fire at once. He was breathless and unable to support himself any longer.

Simeon slumped on his shattered legs, with only the nails in his wrists holding him up. Asphyxiation of his lungs due to lack of oxygen ensued, and he writhed for a short time unable to do anything to give him even a moment of relief. As he knew his time of death was rapidly approaching, Simeon transfixed his stare on Martha and Eleazar with tenderness. At his last moment of life, he turned his gaze towards Jesus' motionless body and seemed to smile. Then Simeon died.

Micah's unrepentant end followed a few minutes later.

With the three criminals now dead, the Jewish religious leaders anticipated their lifeless bodies would be discarded by the Romans in a mass grave. Little did they know that one of their own, a prominent member of the Sanhedrin who had been excluded from the overnight trial of Jesus because they were afraid how he would vote, had gone to Pilate, privately. Joseph of Arimathea had begged that Pilate let him retrieve the body of Jesus and give it a proper burial.

Most crucified criminals were disposed of in a haphazard way and unceremoniously thrown into a mass grave by the Romans. Jesus most likely would have been treated the same way had it not been for Joseph. For whatever reason, maybe because Pilate had announced on six occasions that Jesus was innocent, he agreed to let Joseph take the body and give it a suitable burial.

Soon, Joseph and others at the site of the Cross respectfully lowered Jesus' lifeless body from the executioner's tool and proceeded to hastily prepare His body by anointing it with costly perfumes and ointments. Then they took His body a short distance from Golgotha to a garden spot where Joseph of Arimathea had already created a tomb that he planned to use one day.

No one had ever been buried there.

That's where His disciples laid the body of their slain leader. All of this was done as the religious leaders watched in disgust. They had hoped this fake King would have been dumped in the gravesite of the other criminals and treated with contempt. They were disappointed that Jesus was given any degree of honor at His burial.

Martha and Eleazar were the only ones who followed the Roman soldiers carrying Simeon's and Micah's bodies out of the Dung Gate and down to the Valley of Gehenna, where they were unceremoniously dumped. Martha and Eleazar wept once again because of the callous and criminal way the bodies were mishandled.

Mother and son sullenly walked away from this scene and made their way past the Temple and back towards Jonathan and Abigail's house. They were happy that their two new friends had also just arrived back home. Both ladies shared what happened at their respective burial locations.

Both of them cried again.

Chapter Eighteen

A Zealot for Jesus

THE NEXT MORNING, Martha and Eleazar discussed leaving and going home, but Jonathan and Abigail begged them to stay. They really shouldn't be traveling on the Sabbath and violating the Sabbath's day's journey norm, especially this high day. So they agreed to stay one more day, but that time was dominated at first by a sense of hopelessness and defeat. They talked very little about the events of the day before, and most of their comments were about the ugliness of the Romans and the religious leaders of the Jews who had been so cruel.

Martha was quick to share the testimony of Markus the centurion with her friends. They found that story to be a silver lining on what was otherwise a day illustrated by the darkness that descended at noontime. They also reminisced about every one of the statements from Jesus while He was on the Cross--and what each comment meant.

They even wrote down His exact words.

They didn't want to forget a syllable. They especially enjoyed talking about Jesus' promise that He made to Simeon. All of them marveled at the grace Jesus had shown to Simeon and the assurance they would be together in the afterlife. The more they talked about Jesus and His words the more encouraged and curious they became about what all those things meant.

Still physically and mentally exhausted from the events of Friday, everyone went to bed early even though Shabbat (Sabbath) was over. Martha and Eleazar had to get an early start on their travels back to Nain, where the other children were. No doubt, rumors were spreading wildly in the Galilee, and Martha didn't want her family and friends to worry about them. One of the things she dreaded was telling them the whole story and the cruel death of Simeon. But she could tell them the testimony of what Jesus did for him. Still, thinking about those things again, caused her to cry.

As she had done every morning, Abigail got up before everyone and prepared a very nice breakfast. Eleazar was getting pretty used to this kind of treatment and thought his Mom should take up the habit. The hospitality of Jonathan and Abigail was truly unforgettable. They were wonderful examples of the disciples of Jesus.

Martha and Eleazar were packed and ready to leave when suddenly there was pounding on the door. The last time such a thing happened it was about the bad news that Jesus had been arrested, tried, and condemned to death. Jonathan made his way to the door and this time everyone in the house crowded around to hear the excited visitor. What they heard staggered them and caused them to be completely bewildered. Their friend, who was also a follower of Jesus, reported that before sunrise, Mary Magdalene and several of the other women went to the tomb of Jesus with hopes of additionally anointing His body to slow the decaying process.

They knew nothing about the Roman guards that had been posted at the tomb to keep His disciples from coming and stealing the body. The women talked along the way about how difficult it was going to be to remove the large stone that had been rolled in front of the entrance. The storyteller excitedly reported that when the women arrived at the tomb, the stone had been rolled back so the entryway to the sepulcher was exposed.

And Jesus' body was not there!

They were confused and mortified. As some of the women returned back to where we were hiding along with His eleven Disciples, Mary Magdalene saw Jesus when He walked up to her and began talking to her.

Jesus had Risen from the Dead!

He was Alive!

Mary quickly returned to the Upper Room where we all were and told us her unbelievable experience. It was so unexpected and hard to believe. Peter and John even ran over to Joseph's tomb to see for themselves. It was true. The sepulcher was empty. Jesus was not there. As hard as it is to believe, what Mary Magdalene said appeared to be true.

The four listeners in the house were speechless. Their friend, after delivering this amazing news, excused himself and said he had other disciples to tell. He departed and went at a full sprint to his next destination. Jonathan closed the door and they all stared at one another trying to make sense of this information.

Finally, Jonathan broke the silence, "This is the most amazing thing I have ever heard. Do you think it's true, Jesus is Alive?"

Martha responded first, "Well, if Mary Magdalene claims she saw Jesus, I believe her more than just about anyone else."

Abigail jumped in, "That's true. I believe anything Mary says. But how can it be that He came back to life? We all saw Him die and the Roman soldiers jammed a spear in His heart. How could anyone survive that?"

Jonathan answered, "Oh, there's no doubt He was dead. He didn't survive that crucifixion. So the only answer is He came back to life after being dead. But how?"

Martha said, "Well, we know Jesus raised other people from the dead like Philip and Jairus' daughter, and Lazarus! So we know He could raise up others, but how could He raise up His own dead body?"

The youngest one in the group had the most profound answer. Eleazar declared, "It's because He is God!" Everyone looked in his direction and agreed. Martha even gave her young theologian a bear hug for his insightful response.

After talking for some time about the implications of Mary's discovery, the group could not come up with a better explanation than what Eleazar had said. Jesus must be alive because God validated everything Jesus had said and done by bringing Him back to life. He's God.

With nothing to do at that time, Eleazar suggested they go back home. It was already mid-morning, but they decided to leave even as their minds swirled with possibilities of what might happen next. Martha and Abigail embraced for a long time with emotions of affection and hope related to everything they had experienced together. They all said their heartfelt goodbyes and once again, Martha and Eleazar expressed their deep appreciation and gratitude. They would forever be friends because of the bond they had in Jesus.

Jonathan helped Eleazar prepare their horses and they began their trip back north. Martha and Eleazar pushed the horses a lot harder than normal and they only had to stay over one night along the way and got home late the next evening. It was the fastest they had ever made the trek, but then, they had a lot of exciting things to share. Everything they talked about on the way centered around Jesus and Simeon.

Lydia and John were so happy to see their mother and Eleazar. Even though it was late, they talked way into the night. Ephraim and Martha's mother also eagerly heard their story. Martha tried to lessen the impact of Simeon's death by reassuring everyone what happened between him and Jesus. The rest of the dialogue revolved around all the events and comments of Jesus. They were the first in Galilee, as far as they knew, who were reporting about the Resurrection of Jesus from the dead. They all saw Him expire, and yet, Mary had seen Him after He came back to life.

By the time they were telling the story in Nain, Jesus had presented Himself to all the disciples and the news of His resurrection was sweeping through Jerusalem and all the surrounding areas like wildfire. Finally, at the point of near exhaustion, Martha announced they all needed to get some sleep. That night, both Eleazar and Martha slept better than they had in weeks. Even though Simeon was gone, the assurance of Jesus he would be in eternity with God made everyone in the family believe they would one day see him again. Sleep came swiftly and deeply for the two exhausted travelers.

The next day Martha and Eleazar were able to go over to see Lois and Philip. She had been so anxious about Martha ever since the two had headed to Jerusalem. Lois was so pleased her carrier pigeon message reached Jonathan and Abigail in time to shock Martha and Eleazar. She got real joy out of that situation and categorically refused to take any reimbursement for the cost.

Lois' enjoyment was readily replaced with pain as Martha shared all of the details related to Simeon's arrest and crucifixion. All of them rejoiced about Simeon's encounter with Jesus, even if it was in the last hour of his life. Lois was so glad to hear about Simeon's defense of Jesus and his request for Jesus to remember him. Jesus' response sent shivers down the spines of Lois and Philip. They cried when they heard about the deaths of these two wonderful men. But the excitement returned when Martha shared the news of what happened on the third day following Jesus' burial. And since the news was delivered by their mutual friend, Mary Magdalene, it was just that much more thrilling. Jesus Arose from the Dead.

Hallelujah! That was all Lois and Philip could contribute.

Eleazar interjected, "Hey Philip, you aren't the only one who knows what it's like to die and be raised from the dead." They all laughed at that comment.

Again, Martha offered to pay Lois back for the message she paid for the pigeons with Joshua. But Lois was adamant about not taking anything for that. Then Lois said something that Martha had not considered up to that moment, "Martha, you need to watch your money now, too. You are also a widow." The force of those words really slammed into her. She hadn't let that thought cross her mind, but it was true.

She fought back tears.

Over the course of the next several days, Martha and her family tried to get things in order at their house. Simeon had always provided a comfortable living for them, but from now on things were going to be different. Eleazar and John had both gleaned some carpentry and stone masonry training from their father, but even the oldest didn't consider his skills worthy of a vocation. At best, he would be able to do some odd jobs to help and keep honing his craft.

Within a couple of days, news started arriving in Galilee about the resurrection of Jesus. Indeed, it appeared that Martha and Eleazar's declaration had been the first report in the area, and people had started talking about their amazing claim, but with guarded skepticism. Now it appeared that more and more pilgrims from Jerusalem were making their way home and validating the story. Everyone in Jerusalem was talking about Him coming back to life, and numerous people gave dogmatic testimony that they had seen the resurrected Lord. There was a buzz all around the region. Jesus was alive and, rumor had it, He was coming to Galilee with His disciples. On hearing that news, Martha and Lois and the rest of their families had to go to Capernaum, in case Jesus really did make it back there.

They all agreed that is exactly what they would do.

Sure enough, less than a week later, people were reporting that Jesus had come to Capernaum with some of His disciples, but He was not staying there. He would make appearances and then go somewhere else, as if He disappeared. Martha and Lois agreed they had to try and see Him. So Martha, her three children, Lois and Philip, and Ephraim all packed some provisions and headed down to Capernaum. Martha's mother stayed home as she was not up to the trip.

Martha and Lois decided they would first go about five miles north of Capernaum to Magdala. If they could see Mary Magdalene surely she would have the best knowledge of Jesus' whereabouts and movements. Since they left early from Nain, they made it to Magdala--a distance of about 15 miles--that evening.

It was easy to locate Mary's house because the first person they asked turned out to be her cousin--and everybody knew Mary in that area. Even though it was almost sunset, they proceeded to Mary's home. Rather sheepishly, they knocked on the door and awkwardly waited, wondering if Mary would even remember them.

Mary opened the door and immediately shrieked, "Martha and Lois. I can't believe you came to see me. Oh, please come in!"

Lois responded, "We don't mean to bother you, Mary, and we don't want to impose."

"Don't be ridiculous," Mary quipped, "Come in here." Then, as she focused on Martha, she said, "Oh, I'm so sorry about what happened to your husband. I wanted to talk to you there, but I was trying to be with Mary, Jesus' mother. And you were clearly focused on your spouse. I couldn't believe my eyes when I saw you and discovered the person being crucified next to Jesus was your husband. Simeon, wasn't that his name?"

Martha, with tears welling up in her eyes, answered, "Yes Simeon, and I was devastated to discover he was being executed with Jesus between him and Micah. I couldn't believe anyone would want to crucify Jesus. I, too, wanted to speak to you, but it was obvious you were busy ministering to Jesus' mother."

Mary continued, "Martha, what happened between Jesus and Simeon was the most amazing thing. When Simeon defended Jesus to the other man, and then turned and asked Jesus to remember him that was awesome. Then, when Jesus promised Simeon that day they would be together in Paradise, I shivered with excitement and joy."

Martha said, "Oh, it was the most amazing moment I have ever experienced even though it was at the lowest point of my life. In that instant, Jesus saved Simeon--and me."

"Me too!" chimed in Eleazar. Again, Eleazar's impeccable timing caused everyone to chuckle in an otherwise tense moment.

Mary responded, "The story of Jesus and Simeon on the Cross, and what happened, will be spoken about for all eternity as an example of His mercy and grace. That's why Jesus died. It was to offer salvation to every person, and Simeon was the first to receive His amazing grace and redemption."

Martha started openly weeping, and through her tears answered, "I never thought about that. How awesome will that be?"

Everyone rushed in to console Martha, with John and Lydia leading the way. They embraced their mother. Ephraim was close behind.

Lois moved to advance the conversation and asked Mary, "Is it true, Mary that Jesus is Alive?"

"Absolutely. I've now seen Him five different times since His Resurrection. He is indeed Alive!"

Philip, Eleazar, and John all said simultaneously, "Wow!"

Mary continued with a smile, "He has been here in the area teaching His Disciples, just as He told them He would do following His resurrection. At the times He explained that before His death, they did not understand the meaning of His words. Now, they hang on every comment He makes preparing them for their future ministries. Jesus, and some of His followers, came by my home two days ago to check on me."

"No way," the same three young men said in chorus. This time everyone laughed at their synchronization.

Ephraim boldly asked, "Mary, I've heard so much about you. I'm Martha's father, Ephraim of Nain. Do you know where Jesus might be next? We came down from Nain hoping to see Him and thank Him for all the ways He has affected our lives. Even though I've never met Him, I feel like I know Him."

Mary declared, "It's nice to meet you, Ephraim. To answer your question, I'm not exactly sure when and where Jesus will appear next. Please stay here tonight and take some food. Maybe tomorrow we'll hear about a sighting of Jesus, one that we can go and witness."

Lois exclaimed, "No Mary, we don't want to stay. That was not why we came to visit you."

"Nonsense," Mary responded, "I have this big home, and I'm the only one here, so I insist you let me extend to you hospitality."

They accepted her offer, and it was wonderful. Mary prepared food for them and they ate until they were full. She had multiple rooms for sleeping, so it was easy to arrange beds for the various families, although Eleazar, Philip, and John insisted on sleeping together in the same room. They all continued sharing stories about Mary, Simeon, Jonathan, and Abigail, but the conversation always came back to Jesus. The amazing reality of His resurrection as told by Mary just filled everyone with a sense of wonder. As they went to their various rooms to sleep, everyone was hoping that maybe they would get to see Jesus, too.

The next morning, Mary prepared a feast for breakfast. She had a gift for hospitality. That is why her ministry, along with other significant women, had been to make provisions for Jesus and His traveling Disciples wherever they traveled. Now Mary was pleased that she could help her friends from Cana and Nain.

As the visitors were completing breakfast, they overheard voices in the front part of the house from the courtyard. A few moments later, Mary stood in the doorway and said, "Friends, let me introduce you to Jesus!"

There He stood. Strong. Assured. God-like. As everyone stood there dumbfounded, it was Jesus who spoke first.

"Martha, Eleazar, I saw you on Mount Calvary with Simeon." How did He know their names? How could He have noticed them while going through the ordeal on the Cross? Jesus continued, "I was so eager to see Simeon turn to me and seek forgiveness and eternal life. I was so glad he made that decision and we were united after we both died."

Martha lost her breath at that declaration. Groping to regain her composure, she softly said to Jesus, "Lord, thank You for everything you did for Simeon, and all of us!"

With amazing tenderness, the resurrected Lord said, "It was my joy! I love you, each and every one of you. That is why I came, and that is why I died. I want every one of you to have everlasting life and enjoy eternity with Me in My Father's house." The profundity of His words continued to make everybody stand in stunned silence. He continued, "It's good to see you, Lois and Philip. When I first met you in Nain, things were a little different."

Lois, not knowing what to do or say, genuflected in Jesus' direction and blurted out, "Thank you, Jesus, for giving me back my son. Your gift of life for him forever changed our destiny."

"You are so welcome, Lois. Philip's resurrection really caused quite a stir back then," Jesus said, with a smile. Everyone in the house was smiling too.

Martha once again mustered up enough courage to say, "Lord, how can we serve you? What can we do to express our genuine love and appreciation for all you have done for us? How can we say 'Thank You' for everything?" Tears of joy were running down her face.

Jesus' gentle response was, "Tell everybody the things you have seen and heard and experienced. Tell them, if they will believe in My Name, pray to Me, and ask Me to forgive them of their sins, I will give them the gift of everlasting life in Heaven with Me. It's just like what Simeon said to Me from the cross. And each one of you is my witnesses. Tell them you have seen Me, alive from the dead. Let them know how they can become one of My children by calling upon my Name. Tell them I love them and want them to spend eternity with Me."

With that, Jesus stretched out His hands in a grand gesture of acceptance. It was at that moment they all saw His nail-pierced hands, and Jesus vanished from their sight.

A couple of weeks later, word came throughout Galilee that on the Mount of Olives in Jerusalem, Jesus met with his Disciples one final time. After giving them a final commission and promising them the soon coming of the Comforter, God's Holy Spirit, an amazing thing took place. As His Disciples were there watching, all of a sudden Jesus gradually ascended into Heaven as everyone stared in disbelief.

They peered into the heavens until Jesus disappeared from their sight. And as they watched, two angels suddenly stood by them in shining apparel. The angels promised that this very Jesus was going to return One Day and descend to this very mountain, the Mount of Olives, to return as the true King--the visible Messiah of the Jews.

This incident was shared all over the land of Judea.

Within a couple of years, Lois agreed to move in with Martha and her family. The impetus for that choice was that both Philip and Eleazar had made a major decision. Both young men had surrendered their lives to go and serve their risen Lord as servants of the Gospel. They planned to go to Jerusalem and serve at the local Church there and learn at the feet of the Apostles who were still ministering in Jerusalem.

With Philip's testimony of being raised back to life by Jesus and Eleazar's testimony of witnessing Jesus' grace upon Simeon at the crucifixion, both believed they could be effective ambassadors for the Savior. When they shared their decision with Lois and Martha, at first there was apprehension and perplexity on the part of the widows. But they quickly came to understand the amazing opportunity it was to be evangelists for the cause of Jesus. They could not think of any greater service their sons could do than to give their futures to the One who saved them all.

So they agreed the young preachers could move to Jerusalem with their mother's blessings. Lois sold her home to a distant family relative and moved in with Martha so they could share living expenses and raise John and Lydia during their years of adolescence.

When they were grown, the two ladies would have the resources to live together and share, not just life, but the closest friendship any two widows could have. That relationship was all because of Jesus.

The two young preachers made their way to Jerusalem and initially stayed with Jonathan and Abigail. The Christian couple welcomed these young apprentice missionaries with open arms and gracious hospitality. The two ambitious young students gleaned everything they could about ministry, service, and preaching the Gospel. Both men went on to have dynamic, soul-winning ministries for the witness of Jesus.

Meanwhile, back in Galilee a single, solitary figure still wrestled with the direction of his life. He had forsaken the cause of the Zealot movement because of circumstances that had arisen in his life. But because of one day, and one moment, he had been transformed into a different person. He frequently thought about that day. It was when his heart had pounded in his chest believing a Roman cross was his immediate future. Suddenly, the Romans announced his freedom and he was released to continue living.

The Cross that had been meant for him, ended up with Jesus of Nazareth hanging upon it.

Yes, Barabbas was forever changed by the fact that he should have been crucified, but Jesus took his place. One time years ago, he remembered thinking, "We'll see who really makes a difference in this world, me or Jesus?" Now, Barabbas was firmly convinced that it was Jesus. The frequent question in his heart and mind was...

What am I going to do with Jesus since He gave His life for me?

About the Author

RAY ADAMS has been a Professor at Baptist Bible College in Springfield, MO, for 42 years. He teaches Life of Christ, Old Testament Bible History, History of Baptists, and he has taught classes like, History of Western Civilization, Archaeology, and Bible Geography and Customs. He has also served as an Assistant Pastor at Cherry St. Baptist Church in Springfield, MO, for 40 years. He is a graduate of Baptist Bible College and has two Master's Degrees, one in Ancient Near East History and one in Religious Studies from Missouri State University in Springfield, MO. Ray has worked on several archaeological digs in Israel, most notably with one of Israel's most famous archaeologists, Yigael Shiloh, at the City of David excavations, just south of the Temple Mount area of Jerusalem.

Ray has been married to his wife of over 45 years, Beth, and they have done ministry together all those years. They have two grown sons, Jason who is married to Lisa, and they have four children. Kevin is married to Stacey and they have four daughters. Ray and Beth's eight grandchildren provide extra joy in their lives. They all live and serve the Lord in Springfield, MO, at Cherry St. Baptist Church. Both his sons are Deacons at the Church.

Ray has hosted or led over 20 tours to the Holy Land and Middle East with an archaeological emphasis and significant historical reconstruction of the many sites. Ray often tells his wife that an archaeologist husband is the best kind of husband to have. Because the older she gets, the more interested he is in her. (She's heard it before).

A Zealot's Redemption is Ray's first book to be published. He has contributed to other published works and written numerous articles.